ASHES OF WAR

Dragons of Ares, book 2
With a bonus novella, Artemis's Hunt (Gods of War #1)

USA Today Bestselling Author
Lia Davis

Ashes of War

Dragons of Ares, Book 2

© copyright 2014-2020 Lia Davis

Published by Davis Raynes Publishing Group, LLC

PO Box 224

Middleburg, FL. 32050

Cover Art by Jacqueline Sweet

Formatting by Glowing Moon Designs

All characters in this book are fiction and figments of the author's imagination.

For my own fated mate with love

ASHES OF WAR

DRAGONS OF ARES, BOOK 2

Ashes of War

Ashlynn Blake, minor goddess of the hunt—lethal, beautiful, and able to connect with animals on a psychic level—is the perfect person to place judgment upon an accused dragon. But first she has to prove to the gods that Ty Sullivan is innocent of his crimes. If she fails, she's doomed to lose her heart along with him forever.

Ty's been beaten, scarred, and betrayed by females. He doesn't trust them, can't stand being around them for longer than he or his dragon needs to be. Yet, when he meets Ashlynn, his dragon is ready to mate, but the man believes she's no different than the others.

The Fates have thrown them together, forcing secrets to be told and igniting a passion so fierce it may destroy both of them.

A sh stalked her prey in the shadows, waiting for the low-life SOB to make the wrong turn down a dark alley or at least get a little farther away from humans. Although many of the residents of Serenity Cove knew about the dragons living in the castle in the mountains, they didn't need to know vengeful demi-gods walked their streets.

The demi-god she currently followed cut a sharp left. Her anxiety spiked. The bastard couldn't get away. Not since she'd finally found him, alone. A few blocks from the edge of the market she materialized in front of the demi-god, aka Garrick's—one of the Sons of War and the evil brother—minion. "What's the hurry, Sam?"

Sam stopped dead in his tracks, his mouth fell open and his face turned a bright shade of white. Not bothering to swipe his blond hair from his eyes, he slowly shifted one foot backward as if ready to haul ass. "You…you're dead."

Really? News to her. Twisting, she gave herself a once over for effect before returning her attention back on the shithead. "I don't think so. I'm as alive as you. Oh, did Garrick tell you he killed me? He's always had a crazy sense of humor, don't you think?"

The poor man looked confused for several moments. Then realization lit up his features, his eyes grew round, and he resumed his slow retreat from her. His hands shook at his side. The sour stench of fear rolled off him. Narrowing her eyes, she studied him as he took yet another step back. *Ah, yes.* Her otherworldly glow from spending the two weeks in Olympus healing after being inside Garrick's laboratory when it blew up had given her little secret away. At least it was a secret from the Imperials. None of them knew she was a minor goddess of the hunt.

Perhaps she appeared more like her mother than she believed.

"Oh no you don't," she said when the Imperial turned to run. She lunged and grabbed him by his arm, twisting it around his back, and forced him to his knees. "You'll tell me what I want to know. Are we clear?"

Sam gripped her forearm and squeezed. "Never, bitch."

With a quick jerk she wasn't anticipating, he reached up with his free hand, grabbed the back of her head and tossed her over his shoulder. Her back hit the asphalt, knocking the wind from her lungs. Pain raced up her spine in a hot, searing wave. *Fuck*.

It took her a moment to catch her breath. When she did, she saw the little bastard dart out of the alley. Jumping to her feet and willing her magic to soothe away the aches from hitting the pavement, she chased him as he weaved through the streets of Serenity Cove. Even though it was late enough that most humans were safe in their homes, she cast a cloaking spell to keep those still milling about from noticing things they shouldn't.

The Imperial twisted his upper body around and threw an energy bolt at her. She deflected it and conjured her bow and arrows. The first shot missed, but then she intended only a warning. She wanted information from him.

Information that could lead her closer to finding out how deep Elizabeth fell into Garrick's plans and his army of demi-gods. The daughter of Eros, god of love and desire, had captured and tortured Ty Sullivan—one of Ares's sons and dragon-shifters known as the Sons of War.

And Ash wanted to know why.

During his captivity, according to rumors, he'd gone mad, submitted to his dragon and killed Elizabeth. Eros wanted his head. Ash wasn't about to hand Ty over until she had proof.

Spying a bridge ahead, she teleported to the other side, cloaked herself with an invisibility spell, and waited for Sam. When he reached the end of the bridge, he stopped and turned in a circle, looking for her. She almost laughed and gave herself away. *Simple minds.*

Lowering her invisibility spell, she grabbed Sam by the back of the neck. "Surprise. What did Elizabeth do for Garrick?"

"Who?"

"Don't play stupid with me. Elizabeth, goddess of desire, daughter of Eros. Beautiful blonde with royal blue eyes?"

He shook his head. "I don't know her."

"I'm running out of patience."

The pounding of boots against asphalt made her whirl around, Sam still in her grasp. Two more descendants appeared. "Oh, good. Now we have a party."

Sam went limp in her arms. Glancing down, she saw the small implant behind his right ear and cursed. Dropping the little shit, she focused on the newcomers. The one on her left held up a handheld device, no doubt the trigger to Sam's life.

A deadly leash Garrick used on all his newly created minions.

Well, damn.

Without warning, she thrust two energy balls at the Imperials, both hitting her targets with quick efficiency. Their surprised gazes weren't very satisfying. She'd rather have information she could use before killing them.

A moment later, she materialized in her townhouse

in the center of town and wasn't surprised to see her mother seated on the sofa. "Good evening, *mitera*."

"Why do you waste your time fighting?"

Ash sighed, moved to the fridge and pulled out a beer. She truly loved her mother, but Artemis was a goddess with no understanding of how the mortal world worked. "I'm hunting for info."

"You could get it from the source."

Tilting her head slightly, she studied her mother. Almost a mirror image of herself— long, wavy red hair —the subtle differences in their appearances were in their faces. Ash's was slightly rounder and her eyes were a vivid emerald green while Artemis's were a pale green. By the way the goddess perched on the sofa, her back straight as she picked at her nails, Ash could tell something bothered her. "Say what you came to say."

"Eros demanded Tyson be brought in for judgment sooner."

Fear stilled her heart for a brief moment. "How much sooner?"

"You are to bring him to Zeus in one week."

"What? I had ninety days to research and find proof. I can't bring in an innocent man."

With brows drawn together, Artemis rose and faced her. The goddess's pale green eyes didn't have their usual spark. They were slightly darker than normal like a thin layer of clouds covering the sun, blocking most of the light. "He is a dragon. Rumor says he is not well."

The rumors say…

Bullshit and her mother knew it. Ty might carry the dangerous-man-eating-dragon front well, but he was not insane. He was too clever, too guarded. "I've been close enough to him to know he is sane and has full control over his beast."

"If you are so sure he is innocent, then go to him. Give him no choice but to work with you to find the truth." Artemis stepped closer, took Ash's free hand in hers, and squeezed. "Seduce the dragon if you must. Either way, he will face judgment in seven days."

Artemis dematerialized, leaving Ash alone with her thoughts.

Seduce Ty. That'd be the easy part. Getting him to trust her? That was the challenge of the century.

CHAPTER TWO

Ty stood at the edge of the cliff and stared out over the Atlantic Ocean, his hands fisted by his sides and his dragon pacing beneath his skin. The salty air whipped around him, biting at his chest and arms through his thin, long-sleeved shirt. The cold numbed him, or so he liked to believe. He hadn't slept for two weeks. He doubted he'd be able to rest until he found Ashlynn and brought her back to the mansion.

Where she belonged.

At least his dragon believed she belonged to them. The man wanted nothing to do with the goddess, not for a committed relationship anyway. He didn't trust females. A female lured him to the Imperials—a group of power hungry descendants of the gods controlled by his evil brother, Garrick—and injected him with a potion to make him incapable of shifting into his dragon before they tortured him for their own sick, twisted pleasure.

Not any ordinary female, either. A minor goddess, whom he thought at the time was his mate, or could have been, betrayed him. The endless taunts and physical torture damn near drove him insane. She'd succeeded in breaking his dragon. The man was on the verge of breaking when Zavier found him and brought him home to their brothers. By the time Z found him, Ty's dragon had taken over and killed several Imperials —including the female, a minor goddess of desire and the daughter of Eros.

Z never revealed Ty's state of mind. No, his quiet and private brother just said, "I found him and he's alive. Nothing else matters."

At least Ty believed he'd killed his captors. His memories of the events were unclear at best. In recent months, he'd been plagued with nightmares of his captivity. Yet, the events in the dreams didn't match what he thought happened. He didn't know if they were real or shit his mind conjured. Zavier had said he found Ty naked and pissed off, but unable to shift. It'd been several weeks after his escape before the potion completely left his system and his dragon burst out.

Ever since, they'd waited for the gods to deliver punishment. He'd killed a goddess and would one day have to pay for his crimes. Until then, they would continue to fight Garrick and protect the worlds from falling into his bloodstained hands.

Ty sensed Zavier long before he stepped up beside him. They stood there in silence for several moments before Ty spoke. "I'm taking off for a while."

Zavier nodded. "I figured. We all knew it was coming. We're just surprised you've waited this long."

Of course. He and his brothers were linked together by a blood bond they forged when banished from Olympus. *Also all because of a female.*

A storm daemon and the daughter of Typhon—the gatekeeper to the fiery pits of Tartarus—Sophia had also been Ty's close friend and lover before Garrick claimed her as his mate.

Back then, Garrick was different. He was kind and a male of honor. He was the first to step up and take on any task the gods required…at least until the day Sophia died and Garrick succumbed to his dragon's rage.

Ty found her decapitated body. The child she carried —the little girl everyone thought was Garrick's—gone, stolen from her mother's womb.

When the information of Sophia's death reached Typhon, the daemon threatened to break out of Tartarus and destroy the world as they knew it. As a result, the gods punished the brothers, exiling all of Ares's sons to the human realm, and Sophia had been reborn as a mortal.

The latter news came to their attention a few weeks prior when they met Gwen—Aphrodite's granddaughter —and Elle—the daughter of Nyx, goddess of night. They discovered Gwen's father worked for Garrick, not knowing the dragon's true purpose until it was too late. From the contents of her father's journal, Gwen was able to help them piece together certain facts such as Sophia's rebirth.

After Sophia's death, Garrick became obsessed with the idea Ty killed his mate and stole his child. Soon after their fall to earth, he began searching for descendants and over the years formed the Imperial Order. When the gods got wind of his plot, they charged Ty and his brothers with the task of stopping Garrick from raising another war on the gods.

Five hundred years had passed since their exile from Olympus, a brief period of time for immortal dragons. After a century or so, Garrick fell quiet. It was like he'd given up the fight. However, Ty and the others knew better. A dragon would search until the end of time to gain revenge for his dead mate. About two years ago, Garrick's little army started making appearances in public, not bothering to hide their powers and magical abilities. The attention they drew caused panic among the humans. Stories of daemons and magical beings popped up everywhere. Some villages even put curfews in place.

Markus had stepped up and all but forced their father to give them more information, anything to help them find Garrick's whereabouts and what type of power they faced. Luckily, Ares was just as motivated as they were to stop their brother.

Then Ty let his dick think for him one night while

out having a few beers with Seth and Zavier. Shortly after meeting the bitch, he found himself held captive by Garrick's fucked up band of minions.

Females couldn't be trusted. Period.

Yet here he was, about to chase after Ashlynn, a goddess by all rights of the divine laws and a hunter sent by the gods.

The latter made Ty even more suspicious of the female.

"I'm not sure how long I'll be gone," Ty said to break his destructive train of thought.

Zavier offered him a handheld device. "This has a GPS tracker. If you need us and can't call, for whatever reason, just push the green button."

In another time—before his capture—Ty would've been cocky enough to tell Z where he could stick the GPS. Not anymore. Life was too short, even for an immortal dragon.

He closed his hand around the device. His lips twitched and his heart warmed a little. "This Markus's idea?"

"Gwen's."

The twitch in his lips was back. Markus's female was the only one in a long time Ty felt he could trust. Even he admitted she possessed a pure soul and kind heart. Plus, she was incapable of lying. Being the granddaughter of Aphrodite and one of the Fates meant she was very powerful and Garrick wanted her power.

"Tell Gwen thanks," Ty said, then jumped off the

cliff, shifting at the same time in a flash of red and gold. The burn of his wings extended from his back and the hard change rolled over the rest of his body. The shift into a dragon shot through him like an electric current.

His wings caught an updraft and he was yanked out of his freefall. Leaning into his left side, he turned and flew over the mansion. From there, he spotted the ruins where Ashlynn had last been seen, about a quarter mile away.

He touched down about fifteen feet from the stone remains of Garrick's lab based on the backpack full of shit Gwen brought back. Actually, Ashlynn stuffed random items, from a laptop to flash drives and other devices Ty didn't recognize, in the bag the day the lab exploded, not Gwen. Z was still searching through the computer files and breaking codes. They all hoped the information in the files would give them a one up on Garrick's grand plan to take over Olympus.

Shifting back to his human form and willing clothes to cover his body, he walked to the fallen building. He and Markus combed the area for anything useful to locate their quarries with no luck. It was as if they both disappeared from Earth. Gwen said the building blew up a moment after she was teleported out by Ashlynn, but she didn't know anything else about how it exploded.

He clenched his jaw and fisted his hands. His blood heated in his veins, intensifying his dragon's rage. They needed to find Ashlynn because they refused to believe she was dead. Taking deep, calming breaths, Ty tried to rein in his dragon. "We'll find her."

A twig snapped and he whirled to face the intruder. As soon as the redheaded goddess came into to full view, he froze and his heart pounded. Her hair hung in silky waves around her shoulders and her green eyes sparkled like emeralds. He let his gaze travel down her body. A tight black V-neck sweater and black jeans clung to her modest curves and his palms itched to touch her, to see if she was real.

"Are you going to stand there and stare at me all day?" Ashlynn stepped toward him, her expression a mysterious blend of coyness and invitation.

The dragon snapped his teeth and paced beneath his skin. A hot, dizzying rush of desire filled him. Ashlynn's strawberry scent called to the beast, stirring a fiery need only she could calm. Every day and night she'd been gone, the dragon grew more impatient. Seeing her, being close enough they could touch in two long strides didn't ease some of the darkness he succumbed to over the past weeks. No, being close to her raised a need within him that drove his dragon insane with lust.

The man had no intentions on claiming the female. Not yet, anyway. How did he know she could be trusted?

With a low growl to warn the dragon to back the fuck off, Ty watched her pass him to stare at the ruins. "Where have you been?" he gritted out.

She took a deep breath before answering. "At my mother's. Healing."

"Sounds like she lives nearby."

She turned to look at him, brows raised. "What if she did?"

He growled and took one step forward, wrapped an arm around her waist to jerk her against him. Her body meshed into his, electrifying each nerve ending, and he tried to ignore how perfectly she fit against him. "Don't play with me, female."

A sensual smile lifted her full, kissable lips. "Oh, believe me, I haven't begun to play. Yet."

His dick jerked at the purr in her voice. He inhaled deeply, taking the scents of earth and forest around them. Ashlynn's natural strawberry fragrance intensified, drowning out the other smells, silently telling him she was as turned on as him. With another low growl, he released her and stepped away.

Shaking his head to clear his thoughts, he gave her his back, not wanting her to see just how much she affected him. No, he couldn't allow her to ever see his weakness, or any others he hid from the world. He needed to stay away from her or he might do something stupid—like fuck her and claim her as his dragon wanted.

"Why are you here?" he bit out.

"Same reason as you. I was looking for you."

He glared at her over his shoulder. "What makes you think I was looking for you?"

She stared back at him, arms folded over her chest, and shrugged, but a smile lifted one corner of her lips. "I'm a goddess, remember?"

Like he needed a reminder. The otherworldly glow of her skin told him she wasn't lying about healing. "Artemis pull you out?" He nodded to the pile of stone.

Her gaze flicked to the ruins. "Yes. She and I wounded Garrick pretty badly, although I don't remember much after I teleported Gwen to safety. How is she?"

He turned to face her fully, thrown off slightly by her short ramblings. "Gwen is well and safe with her mate."

"That's good. I like her."

Ty's lips twitched again and he decided he really needed to get the muscle spasms looked at. "Gwen kind of grows on you the more you're near her."

Ash blinked at him and for a moment he thought she was about to give some kind of smart-assed response. Instead she looked away after a few moments to scan the area. "Look, I need to talk with you, but not here."

She pulled a slip of paper from her front jeans pocket and handed it to him. "That's the address to my townhouse in Serenity Cove."

Then she dematerialized.

Ty read the address and growled. How long had she lived in the same town as they while she worked for Garrick?

Ash materialized inside her townhouse, her heart still stuttering and her body flushed from being so close to Ty. Gods, he looked good, and his scent... It clung to her, seeping into her mind and skin. Tamping down rising desire, she walked to the fridge and jerked it open to grab a bottle of water.

What she was about to do went against all logic of being Ty's judge and jury, however, Ash couldn't see any other way to prove his innocence in regard to Elizabeth's death. No one in Olympus could tell her anything other than he had done it. Yet, Ash's gut told her there was more to the story, secrets the gods didn't want to reveal.

Her mother's words rang inside her head. *Seduce the dragon if you must. Either way, he will face judgment in seven days.*

A heavy knock sounded on the door, making her jump. Squeezing her eyes shut, she took a deep breath then pushed off the counter. She yanked the door open and strode to the living room, allowing Ty to follow her inside the townhouse. Her hands shook, but it wasn't from fear. No, she didn't fear him. She wanted him so badly it hurt to be close to him.

Her only explanation for the reaction was she'd lost her edge, or perhaps she was just losing her mind. "Would you like a beer?" she asked, peeking over her shoulder.

He shook his head and crossed his arms over his broad chest, pulling his long sleeved shirt tighter against his muscles. "What do you need to talk to me about?"

She held her tongue like she'd done at the ruins of Garrick's lab. Fighting with Ty would only make her job more difficult. She needed his trust and cooperation.

Even though she could sense the darkness within him, she also picked up on his light—the little inner peace he clung to. Meeting his stare, she said, "I need your help, but I know you don't trust me."

The muscles in his temples flexed. "I trust no one but my brothers."

Yes, she'd known that. Steeling her back, she stared into the dark lenses of the shades he always wore. "My true mission is to find Elizabeth's killer and pass judgment."

He didn't move, just stood there staring at her through those damned shades. "Why are you telling me?"

She closed her eyes briefly before she sat on the sofa facing him. "I need you to trust me and help me. Lying to you about my true purpose would give you more reason not to trust me. I also need you to believe I'm on your side."

He let out a humorless laugh and unfolded his arms. "So coming clean is supposed to make me trust you? You have to earn my trust, female."

She didn't need this shit. She stood, stepped into his space, and glared into the lenses of his shades. "Fine, then. You can leave. I'll get my answers from Garrick instead."

She pushed past him, but he stopped her by grabbing her upper arm. Then he leaned close, his lips barely brushing her ear. "I didn't say I wouldn't help you."

"I can't work with someone who doesn't trust me."

She swore she saw the corner of his lips twitch before he said, "I learned a long time ago that the people closest to you can screw you, so don't take it personally."

Jerking her arm free from his grasp, she walked to the refrigerator and pulled out two beers. She rounded the corner and ran into Ty. He slid his hands up her arms and held her in place. For a moment, she couldn't breathe. The intensity of his sage scent and the power surrounding him made her weak in the knees and heat pooled between her legs.

A dark brow rose over the top rim of his shades. "We have to take care of one small issue first."

She swallowed, hating the weakness this man and his damn dragon created in her. "What's that?"

He pressed his cheek to hers, bit lightly on her ear lobe, and whispered. "I want to fuck you until you scream."

Well, damn.

Beers forgotten, she dropped them, the bottles bounced on the carpet and rolled to *clink* against the coffee table leg. Wrapping her arms around his neck, she fisted her hands in his hair and kissed him.

CHAPTER THREE

Ash bit down on Ty's lower lip, drawing a low, husky half-growl, half-groan from him. He pressed his hard, jean covered erection into her abdomen. "Are you sure you want to play with a dragon?"

She drew back to study the dark shades, desperately wanting to snatch them off his face so she could see his eyes. Yet she couldn't do it, couldn't take the sense of security or whatever he clung to away from him. He'd have to be ready to allow her access to all of him. "I've *been* ready to play with you."

"I'm not a gentle lover."

"I don't need gentle right now."

A slight glow flickered from behind the lenses as he walked her backward until he pinned her against the wall. She tugged at his shirt until he backed away then yanked the thing over his head and let it fall to the ground. Following her lead, he had her sweater removed in a flash. Whether it was by magic or not, she didn't care. Then, he ripped her pants off.

She bit his ear and snarled. "I liked those jeans."

He sucked in a breath and pressed his still clothed lower body into her. "That's too bad."

A shudder rippled through her at the sound of his arrogant, yet sexy, husky tone. She scored his shoulder blades with her nails and rotated her hips against him, drawing another growl from him.

When she slid one hand down his back to the waistband of his jean, he gripped her wrist and jerked it over her head, pinning it to the wall. Scorching desire raced in her veins, making it impossible to think of anything beyond having him inside her.

With his free hand, he tore her panties off then undid his jeans. She stifled a cry as he freed his cock and teased her clit. Her skin was on fire and way too sensitive to his every touch. Removing his shades, he tossed them on the coffee table behind him and dipped his head to trail kisses down her neck. When he reached the bend where it connected to her shoulder, he bit down. Sharp pain turned to intense pleasure, making her come on the spot.

He slid inside her, filling her, stretching her. She lifted her legs, wrapping them around him and allowing him to go deeper. Gasping, she laid her head against the wall and arched her back.

Ty thrust into her slowly at first, then faster, building

until she screamed as her climax slammed into her. His body went taut right before he roared his own release.

TY RESTED his head against Ashlynn's shoulder, every muscle relaxed and his dragon fully sated for the first time since before his capture. That alone should've been enough to make him leave. All he had to do was back away, put his cock back in his pants and grab his shirt then leave. Yet, he couldn't find the mental strength to do it.

Pulling out of Ashlynn's tight pussy, he lowered her to her feet and turned his back to grab his sunglasses from the coffee table. The rustling of clothes told him she was dressing, but he didn't dare look at her because his damn dragon wanted to bond with her, claim her as his mate. *The damn beast.*

"I killed Elizabeth," he said to break the awkward silence.

"I don't believe you did."

He whirled around, glad she was fully dressed as she sat on the sofa and watched him. The jeans he'd ripped off her still a pile of denim where he discarded them. "How can you be sure?"

She averted her gaze and studied the carpet for a few moments before answering. "Remember, I gave my word not to lie to you because I need your trust in order to find out what happened to Eros's daughter." She inhaled, then exhaled slowly. "I'm a minor goddess of the hunt, but you already know that. Did you know I have the ability to connect with the animal world?"

His pulse slowed and a sick feeling of dread churned in his gut. "I guess it comes with the title. I sense a 'but' in there."

She lifted her green gaze to his. "I can sense your dragon. I'm guessing I could connect with him like I can with other animal species."

"You guess?"

"I haven't tried. It'd be a violation of your free will."

He would have laughed, but the way she held eye contact and remained relaxed told him she spoke the truth. "Your *gift* tells you I'm innocent, even though you haven't used it on me?"

Her eyes narrowed and she worked her jaw as if choosing the right words. Ty suppressed his amusement. "It's hard to explain. I just know. I've known since seeing you at the mansion."

"Try to explain."

"It's more like a knowing. I could sense your dragon as well as your brothers' dragons. Even though you hold onto the darkness more, I don't feel evil within you like I do with Garrick. Your twisted brother has the capability to kill for his own enjoyment. It's sickening. You don't. You kill out of necessity or self-defense." She paused and stared at him.

He tried to think back on the day Zavier tore through

the place he'd been held, but couldn't remember. Everything played in his mind like broken pieces of a bad movie. Nothing made sense. Letting out a sigh, he turned to pace to the window and scanned the streets below. "I don't remember much after my dragon took control of my mind. Zavier said Elizabeth was dead when he arrived."

Fabric sliding across the leather couch made him turn his head enough to watch Ashlynn from the corner of his eye. She stood and advanced to stand next to him. "It is possible Garrick killed her and made you believe you did it."

He angled his body so he faced her and leaned against the window frame. "How?"

She watched the people mill about the busy street below. "Garrick has potion makers working for him in the Imperial Order. He also has a couple of magic weavers. He could have used one or both to erase your memories enough so you wouldn't know if you did it or not. My guess is he counted on the fact you'd take the blame, given your state of mind."

He let out a low growl of annoyance. "What would you know about my state of mind?"

She tilted her head back slightly to study him and frowned. "I was given some details before I was sent on the mission. I was told you'd submitted to your dragon and went insane, but that day at the mansion—outside your room—I didn't sense any insanity. I felt anger, rage, and mistrust. That is when I decided I needed more information. I believe someone else killed Elizabeth and wanted you to take the fall for it."

He cursed low and pushed away from the window to pace the apartment. Garrick had motive to do it and blame him. "Garrick blames me for Sophia's death."

Ashlynn tilted her head and watched him. "How so?"

Ty stopped pacing and faced her. "Because her unborn child was mine."

She opened her mouth, closed it, and her eyes darkened slightly. "But they were mated, weren't they?"

Ty nodded. "Sophia and I were close friends. About a month before Garrick claimed her as his, we spent a weekend together. She said she was attracted to both of us, but wanted to be sure which one of us was her true mate."

He fisted his hands and clenched his teeth. "I believe she played both Garrick and me. She wanted both of us, but neither one of us wanted to share. Plus, I didn't love her the way Garrick did."

"So she got pregnant by you and mated Garrick."

"Exactly. She got both of us."

Ashlynn let out a breath. "No wonder you don't trust women. I wouldn't either."

He shrugged. "What do you suggest we do now, goddess?"

She rolled her eyes and glanced back out the window, then her body tensed. "We have to take care of our visitors first."

He was about to ask what she meant when the front door blew open and daemons rushed inside, throwing energy bolts at them. His heart stopped for a brief moment when Ashlynn dropped to the floor, blood soaking her shirt.

He roared and thrust fireballs at the daemons in rapid succession. They screamed as flames engulfed their bodies, then *poofed* into black ashes. Ty took a step toward Ashlynn when Eros materialized in front of him.

The god of desire was the opposite of his mother, Aphrodite, in many ways. He had short black hair, but the same blue eyes. Ty growled, allowing his dragon to surface in case he was needed to fight the god. "What do you want, Eros?"

"I want you to suffer like I have. Thanks for the tidbit about Amissa being your daughter, not Garrick's. Now I know how to repay you for my loss." Eros dematerialized.

Fuck no. Amissa. He needed to get to her and warn her guardian.

Ty rushed to Ashlynn, scooped her up in his arms, and flashed them to his beach house in Oregon.

CHAPTER FOUR

A sh opened her eyes and froze. She wasn't in her townhouse. As she sat up, she groaned at the dull ache in her chest. Seeing the daemons entering the building, then breaking in her door flashed through her mind.

She fisted her hands. *How dare they burst into my home?* Fucking bastards hit her with an energy bolt strong enough to put a dragon down.

She scanned the room and noticed it was a bedroom. A plain room—white walls, white ceiling, and white mini-blinds—with no art on the walls or personal effects anywhere. At least the floors were a dark hardwood, which warmed up the room and kept it from looking overly sterile. A moment later, the door opened and Ty entered carrying a tray of food.

He lifted his head in her direction and smiled. Her heart skipped several beats as her body warmed. *He has no right to be so damned hot, yet so irritating at the same time.* "I do believe that is the first time I've seen you smile."

He set the tray down on a small table by the window, his smile fading. "Come, eat. I'll tell you everything I remember and answer your questions."

Suspicion crawled up her spine and whispered in her ear as she studied him a little closer. His words were clipped and a muscle in his jaw flexed. Something had happened. She slid from the bed and made her way to the table. She could barely make out the shapes of his irises through his shades. It was enough she could tell the right one wasn't human, instead forever stuck as the dragon's eye. Reaching up, she touched the rim of the glasses, but he grabbed her wrist before she could remove them.

"Don't," he growled.

She tsked. "I've already seen what's behind them."

"Then why bother now?"

She shrugged, but didn't avert her gaze. *Honesty, Ash. You promised him the truth.* Did it really mean she had to reveal her feelings to him? If she kept him at a distance, then the whole "seduce him" thing wouldn't work. "I'm curious. Everything about you fascinates me."

He stared at her through those shades. She thought he was going to push her away and go on the defensive. However, he released her wrist and waited. Slowly, she removed the sunglasses.

His right eye—the dragon's eye—was crimson with streaks of gold running from the elongated pupil to the outer edge of the irises. The area around the eye was heavily scarred. In random places, the skin had been replaced by red scales with gold undertones.

She reached up and hesitantly touched his scarred skin with her fingertips. He flinched but didn't pull away, just continued to watch her.

"Garrick did this?"

"Elizabeth did."

Anger rose up in Ash and she wanted to go back in time and kill the female herself. "The bitch got what she deserved."

Sitting down at the table, Ash lifted the cover from the plate and her mouth watered. Scrambled eggs sprinkled with cheddar cheese piled in the middle with buttered toast on one side and bacon on the other. "This smells divine. I didn't know you could cook."

He covered her hand with his, drawing her gaze to him. She smiled in satisfaction when he didn't replace his sunglasses. Her smile was short-lived. When he linked his fingers with hers, a sad expression clouded his features. "After I killed the daemons, Eros popped in. He knows about my daughter and is looking for her as we speak."

Her heart sank to her belly. "She's alive? Why the hell didn't you tell me?"

He narrowed his gaze and the muscles in his jaw flexed. "I've been in contact with her guardian for the last few years after I dragged the information out of Ares. My father apparently found Amissa as an infant and hid her from the gods and me."

"How did you find out?"

"I overheard the nymphs talking and confronted Ares."

Ash picked up her fork and dipped it in the eggs, not surprised that Thea and Ariel—two of Aphrodite's handmaidens—gossiped about what went on in Olympus and the rumors they heard there. "Who is her guardian?"

"Her current one is her second. Ares said he placed her in a griffin clan where she was raised and taught to shift into her dragon and use her powers for self-defense. Cyrus stepped in about five years ago as her official protector." He frowned again, then released her hand and leaned back in his chair.

She knew Cyrus. He'd come to Olympus many times when she was a child through her adult life to assist the gods on many tasks. "Cyrus is a good male."

Ty glared at her. "I've called him to come by so I can brief him on the situation."

Ash nodded and took a bite of her eggs and sighed. "These are really good."

His lips twitched, making him look even sexier than he already did. "Where do you want to begin?"

She thought about it. Knowing Elizabeth was responsible for his scars and damage to his eye made Ash more determined to help clear his name. There was no way she'd let him face death without justification. They just had to prove to the gods that the bitch had turned against them. "What do you remember about Elizabeth? Like, her state of mind. Was she willingly aiding Garrick?"

He drew his brows together as if in thought. "Was she sane? Yes, very much so. Seth, Zavier and I were at pub when I met her. I was looking to blow off some steam and have a little fun."

When he shifted his gaze back her, Ash averted hers, not wanting him to see the spike of jealousy in her eyes. Although he could probably pick it up in her scent. To her relief, he didn't call her on it and continued speaking. "When she got me alone outside the bar, she injected me with some kind of serum. I'm not sure how she got me to Garrick's lab. She most likely had help or maybe she teleported me. Everything from there is bits and pieces. I remember her and Garrick arguing, but I don't know what about."

Ash took another bite of eggs, then a drink of milk. "How long ago was this?"

"About three years."

She hadn't been in the Order at the time. "Garrick hates when his Imperials argue with him. He fears they will go against him, so he keeps them under a spell to obey him. Plus he has many of them implanted with a chip to track them and disable them."

"Disable them?"

"The device sends an high electric pulse straight to

their heart when they show signs of betrayal. Anyway, either Elizabeth was immune to the spell or she promised him inside info."

His forehead creased and he slowly nodded. "Like she had her own objective. What about the implant?"

"Garrick wouldn't risk placing one in her because of connection to her father. Eros would know as soon as his daughter's been implanted, which leads me to believe she had something he wanted or promised him something. But I don't know of any reason why she'd go against her father and the rest of the gods. She was raised in Olympus like me, pampered and cooed over. All the children back home were."

Ty's face lit up and he sat up in his seat. "She was a minor goddess of desire, right?"

"Yes. Why?"

"Desire isn't always sexual."

For the love of the gods, why didn't I think of that? "Greed and envy can come with desire. She could have wanted more than the life her father gave her, more power. I remember how she obsessed about the powers you and your brothers held."

Ty shook his head and stood. "It's great in theory, but we need proof."

Ash sighed and set down her fork. "I know. Is there anything else you remember?"

"No."

She stood and placed a hand on his forearm. "Can you try to remember? I know I'm asking you bring back memories your mind buried, but I'm not going to let you face a death penalty."

He narrowed his eyes at her. "Why not, goddess?"

She squared her shoulders and met his stare. "Because my heart would break if you died."

He titled his head, slightly. "What are you saying?"

You are mine. She couldn't speak the words. She wasn't sure if she'd be able to tell him that every time she was near him the need to bond with him grew stronger. If she had to live the rest of her existence loving him from a distance, she'd do so. But to watch him die for a crime he didn't commit? It would break her.

Relief washed over her when a knock sounded on the front door, drawing his attention away from her. He grabbed his sunglasses from the table and slid them in place. Leaning into her, he growled, "We will finish this conversation later."

She was afraid of that.

TY OPENED the door and stepped aside to allow Cyrus and Amissa to enter his small beachfront home in Seaside, Oregon. Cyrus nodded to him as he passed, then he gaze fell on Ash and a wide smile replaced his normally serious features. Ty tracked the griffin as he advanced toward Ashlynn while Ty bent to allow Amissa to kiss him on the cheek. Although he trusted

Cyrus like a brother, he didn't like the other male so close to Ash. Which confused the hell out of him.

Ash didn't belong to him, so why did he give a shit who she hugged?

Cyrus scooped Ashlynn up in a tight embrace. Ty growled and closed in on them. Ashlynn narrowed her eyes at him and pushed out of the griffin's hold. Before Ty could say anything, Amissa stepped forward, arms crossed. "Who are you?"

Ashlynn smirked. "Ashlynn, daughter of Artemis."

Amissa drew back slightly as if surprised then turned to Ty. He held out a hand and when she placed hers in it, he explained. "Ashlynn is here to help me with some things."

"Cyrus wanted me to stay home, but I wanted to see you. Why haven't you come to visit?" She pursed her lips and glared at him.

Ty glanced to Cyrus then Ashlynn and sighed. He really didn't want Amissa brought into it. The less she knew the safer she was, or so he told himself. But his daughter was as stubborn as he and her mother. "Amissa, please sit and don't speak until I'm done explaining."

She stared at him for a few moments, her jaw working. Finally she paced to the couch and sat. Cyrus chose to stand against the wall behind her. Ty removed his shades and scrubbed a hand over his face. He met Amissa's stare and told her how he got the scars and why his eye would never shift back to human. "I killed the female responsible and it turned out she was Eros's daughter. Now the god of desire wants me sentenced to death. That's why Ashlynn is here."

Amissa jerked forward, but Cyrus rested his hands on her shoulders before she could lunge for Ashlynn. "She can go back and tell them it was self-defense."

Ashlynn shook her head. "It's not as easy as it sounds. The gods' law is different from the human ones you are used to. I was sent to bring him in or find evidence of his innocence."

Ty dropped into the chair directly across from Amissa. "We were attacked at Ashlynn's apartment and Eros paid me a little visit. He overheard me tell Ash about you and now he is looking for you. Your life is in danger because you are my daughter. You must go back to the griffin clan until this is cleared up."

Amissa shook her head and folded her arms. "I'm not going anywhere."

"Amissa," Ty and Cyrus growled at the same time.

She pressed her lips together and stared at Ty. Defiance settled into her features, reminding Ty of Sophia. As much as he wanted to hate the storm daemon, she had been his friend. Amissa jiggled her foot. "I'm not leaving. I'll stay and fight. I finally found my father and, damn it, I want to fight to keep him."

"Knowing Cyrus, I guessing you've gone through some brutal training?" Ashlynn broke her silence.

Amissa's lips lifted and she glanced at Ashlynn.

"Every freaking day from the time he took over my guardianship."

Ashlynn met Ty's glare before asking her next question. "What about your powers?"

Amissa shifted in her seat. "I can shift into a dragon."

Ashlynn paced to the window and said, "No, I mean the power you got from your mother."

"I can control the elements, but I've never tested the extent of them."

Cyrus spoke next. "We were always afraid she'd draw attention to herself, so we haven't explored her daemon side."

Ty understood and was grateful for Cyrus's knowledge of gods and daemons who could track Amissa by the use of her powers. Not only did Ty have to keep his daughter's whereabouts a secret from Eros, but he also had to keep Garrick off her tail. Because his brother believed Amissa was his daughter.

"You're not fighting. I need you to return to the clan."

His daughter lifted her chin slightly and glared at him. "I'm not hiding out while you face a death sentence."

They stared at each other until Ash spoke. "She'd be safe at the mansion and close enough to you. I agree, she's not ready for this fight. At least at the mansion she'll be able to train and learn the limits of her powers without alerting Garrick or anyone else who is searching for her."

Ashlynn had a point. He didn't have to like it, but he couldn't argue her logic. The mansion was warded from outside threats, something Zavier and Markus put into place after discovering the laboratory less than a mile away. A year ago they wouldn't have bothered. They would have welcomed the bastard with opened arms. Not now. They had two females living in the mansion, both of which were descendants from the gods and on Garrick's demi-god collection list. Gwen was mated to Markus and there was no way the male would allow anything happen to her.

Still, Garrick never made an attempt on storming the mansion. Why? Ty could only think his brother had plans that needed them all alive in order to execute his evil plot.

"Fine," he growled, then locked gazes with Amissa. "You will do as you're told and not leave the mansion without an escort."

She pursed her lips and fisted her hands. When she opened her mouth to speak, Cyrus placed his hands on her shoulders again. Releasing a sigh, she rolled her eyes. "Deal. But when I'm strong enough, I'm fighting by your side to stop this war."

Ashlynn sat down on the arm of Ty's chair. He had to force his gaze from her, and ignore her scent. His dragon wanted nothing more than to take her until they were panting and exhausted. Shaking out of the desires to claim the female, he focused on Amissa and refrained from pushing Ash off his damned chair arm.

"What do you know about the pending war?" Ash asked, making him instinctively reach out to caress the ends of her hair. She calmly swept the strands over her shoulder, out of his reach.

What the fuck was wrong with him? It was like he had no sense of self-control when the female was around.

"I know Garrick is building an army."

Cold dread sliced up Ty's spine. He'd never told her. Glancing to Cyrus, he noted how the griffin's expression remained unreadable. *Interesting.* "How do you know that?"

She averted her gaze and wrung her hands in her lap. "I was confronted by a couple of descendants in the market about a week ago. They said Garrick would be happy to know a female dragon lived here. After Cyrus killed them, I demanded he tell me everything."

Fuck. Shit just kept getting better and better. "Why didn't you call me? Better yet, why didn't you take her back to the clan?"

Cyrus let out a low growl. "She is *your* daughter."

Amissa stood and threw her hands up. "I'm not a child! I'm in this whether you like it or not, it all started with my mother…"

Ty straightened. "What do you mean?"

Ash stood and walked to the window. "The archives

say it was a storm daemon who started the first uprising."

"Sophia wouldn't have done that." Ty was sure of it. Well, almost. The storm daemon was *capable* of doing it, but she had no reason, not to his knowledge anyway, to wage war on the gods.

Ash turned back to face them. "Maybe not, but someone wanted everyone to believe she did."

"But who?" Amissa asked.

That's what Ty wanted to know. Sophia was many things, but she wasn't a power hungry monster. "I don't know, but we'll find out."

Ash made a noise in her throat before reminding them of the immediate task at hand. "First we have to clear Ty's name and make sure the gods don't kill him."

CHAPTER FIVE

"You want a what?" Zavier smiled at the irritated growl coming from the other end of the call. It was a legitimate question since it was Ty whom he was talking to.

"I. Want. A. Magic weaver. Is that plain enough for you? Eros is breathing up my ass and has threatened Amissa. I need answers and if they are locked away with my memories, then I need them unlocked or what the fuck ever." Ty took a breath and fell silent.

"Well if you explained that the first time, I wouldn't have questioned you. Magic weavers are very rare and most have gone into hiding because of bastards like Garrick, among other daemons." Zavier brought up Google search and typed in *magic shops*. One thing about weavers, they couldn't stop practicing spell making. Magic and other occult shops were the perfect places to find a weaver.

"There are a couple of spell shops a few miles outside of town. I'll send Gwen to check them out." Zavier printed out the addresses for four shops within a hundred miles from Serenity Cove.

"How long will this take?" Z didn't blink at his brother's impatient tone. He was used to it and understood. "I'll have her, and most likely Markus, ready to go right away. They'd have to travel the human way, to ensure Garrick or the humans do not discover them. My best guest, if we're lucky, would be about a week. But I think that is pushing it."

The sound of heavy, yet small, footsteps made him twirl around and meet the annoyed glared of Elle—aka Danielle Roberts, daughter of Nyx and his biggest distraction. "Ty, man, we'll find one for you. You should come home and bring Amissa and Cyrus with you."

"No, it's safer here for now."

"Okay. I'll call when I have something." Zavier hung up the phone and folded his arms at the dark haired goddess in front him.

She stepped inside his computer room, which recently shrunk in size allowing Elle to have her own studio where she could paint or sculpt or whatever artistic thing she could come up with. The decision to share his space with her had been a mistake. The female was impossible. She was messy, leaving paintbrushes scattered about and the damned paint jars weren't even organized by color. It totally fucked with his OCD. Yet, he couldn't seem to stay away from her. "Can I help you, Elle?"

"Have you seen my fan brush?"

"Your what?"

She fisted her hands. "Fan brush. It's a paint brush shaped like a handheld fan."

He stepped to the curtain, which divided their areas and flung it open, then stormed over to the workbench and pointed to the wall. "I organized them by size. I don't understand how you can find anything in all this mess."

The muscle in her jaw flexed. "It's my mess and I know exactly where everything is."

She pushed past him and yanked the brush from the hook and slammed it to the table next to a painting he hadn't noticed until just then. His heart stopped briefly and all he could do was stare at the images on the canvas. "You dreamt this?"

Her shoulders dropped. "Two nights ago."

He faced her and an ache formed in his chest. She had dark circles under her eyes and her hair was twisted in a messy bun on top of her head. Reaching out, he brushed a finger across her cheek. She jerked away from the touch, which only made him advance and grab her into a tight hug. "You haven't slept since then?"

She pressed her paint-stained hands to his chest. His skin under his black, cotton shirt burned from the touch. After a moment she relaxed into him. "No. I felt his pain. I've never done that before."

Zavier picked her up and carried her to the sofa on his side of the room. Sitting, he cradled her against his chest and stared at the painting. She'd captured Ty towered over a dead female inside some kind of lab or torture room—Zavier couldn't tell which due to the lack of details in the background of the image. He had a hunch that once it was finished, it'd resemble the room where he'd found Ty. Standing in front of Ty, Garrick held a large dagger that looked identical to the one Hades guarded in the Underworld. The dagger was supposed to be a one of a kind and the only thing that could kill an immortal dragon or a god.

Pulling out his cell from his pocket, he snapped a picture and texted it to Ty and Markus.

TY STARED at the phone screen, frozen in place. Anger mixed with confusion as he studied the painting. No one but Zavier knew the details of his captivity and Z didn't know much beyond what he'd walked into.

Yet, here it was, a moment in time ripped out of the day Z found him—only it wasn't like he remembered. He didn't recall Garrick being there or possessing the divine dagger. The more he stared at the photo, the more familiar the scene became. A dull ache formed in the middle of his forehead, then images flashed through his mind.

His vision blurred as he scanned the room. Too clean. Everything was too clean and smelled of beach and something else he couldn't place. A shuffle of feet against concrete sounded from behind him, but he couldn't turn to see who it was.

"Hello?" His voice sounded hoarse and his throat ached from screaming during the last torture session. He shuddered at the memory. They'd bound his legs and arms with magically enhanced chains he couldn't break and something dripped down on his face. Drop by slow, agonizing drop, the mystery fluid hit his eye, burning and eating away at his skin.

"Don't speak. They will hear you." The male voice came from behind him.

"Who are you?" he asked in a lower tone.

"One of your brothers. Tyson, it's Nik..."

The male's voice cut off the instant the door opened. A moment later Elizabeth's face filled Ty's vision. She grinned as she took the time to appreciate her handiwork on his face.

Ty dropped his phone and clenched his head as sharp pain sliced through his skull. He stumbled backward. Rage filled his veins and his dragon roared in his mind, making the headache intensify.

Cool feminine fingers wrapped around his forearm and he shot out one hand, grabbing her by the throat and twisting to slam her back against the wall. A fierce growl erupted from him, shaking the house.

A male spoke from a few feet behind him. "Ty, what the hell is wrong with you?"

Cyrus? Why is the griffin here? Confusion moved into his already clouded mind. Shaking his head, he focused on the female he trapped against the wall. Emerald eyes set into a rounded, creamy-toned face stared back at him.

"What trick is this?" he growled.

"No trick. It's Ashlynn, remember?" She removed her hand from his arm and placed her palm against his heart. "Feel me? I'm here. You're here. We're safe."

Footsteps behind him shuffled to the door, making him jerk his head toward them. Ashlynn's hand touched his cheek and she continued to speak in soft soothing tones. "Let them go and focus on me."

He returned his gaze to hers and frowned. "Ash?"

She smiled. "Are you back?"

Yes, no…where in Hades did he go? Unsure if any of it was real, he glanced over his shoulder in time to see Cyrus usher a protesting Amissa out the door. Then he met Ash's gaze and watched how the deep emerald green seemed to lighten, then darkened as he traced her bottom lip with his thumb. Her cheek blushed as her skin heated. He dipped his head and brushed his lips across hers.

A jolt of familiar, sensual energy rushed through him and straight to his cock. He flattened his body to Ashlynn's and deepened the kiss. Her tongue thrust inside his mouth, tangling with his. He released her throat and roamed her body with his hand, needing to feel her. When he didn't find bare skin, he ripped her clothes from her in one swift motion.

Breaking the kiss, he lifted his head to gaze into her eyes. "I'm back, goddess."

She smiled and nipped at his bottom lip. "Good. Now fuck me."

He should walk away. Leave the female alone. They couldn't be trusted. Yet, he couldn't make his feet move, or make his hands stop roaming over her clothed body, seeking bare skin.

Ashlynn was a drug to him and his dragon. They couldn't get enough of her.

He lifted her up in his arms and carried her to the bedroom. Against his better judgment, he was going to savor every moment. Laying her down on the bed, he hovered over her, studying her. She was beautiful. Her long red hair fanned out over the white comforter. "What is it about you?"

She pressed a finger to his lips. "Stop thinking. Take what you need."

The fire in her green eyes dimmed slightly, inviting compassion and a promising passion. Yet so had Elizabeth's gaze, he recalled, the night he saw her at the bar. The same night she lured him to Garrick and his torture began.

Pain shot through his skull. He gripped his head

with both hands and rolled to his back. Ashlynn's cool fingers brushed across his skin as she began to message his scalp. Instantly, the headache eased. "How do you do that?"

Continuing to rub circles on his head and temples, she shrugged. "I'm not sure."

Her scent said she lied, but somehow it didn't bother him. In fact, he feared he already knew the answer. Neither of them were ready to admit it. The feelings and the draw toward her were similar to what he'd felt with Elizabeth. Only with Ashlynn the pull was stronger, the desire more intense. "Ashlynn?"

"Call me Ash, please."

"Ash." He liked the sound of her name.

She sighed and pushed off the bed and moved toward the door, then turned. "We need to call a meeting with your brothers. We have six days to figure this shit out."

He stilled and scowled. "Six days?"

"Eros has moved up your judgment."

Rising from the bed he stalked to her, hands fisted and irritation building. "When were you going to tell me?"

She placed a hand on his chest and pushed. "Don't go dragon on me. I was going to at my townhouse before we were interrupted, then Amissa and Cyrus came by. It slipped my mind."

He should call her out on the oversight, but he

couldn't. Shit just seemed to be coming at them ninety miles a second. "Fuck."

"Yep." She pivoted and left him standing in the doorway, watching her ass as she stormed down the hallway.

Fuck.

CHAPTER SIX

Garrick entered his office at the east coast headquarters of the Imperial Order and froze at the sight of Eros gazing out the window. Without turning, the god of desire spoke in a deep raspy tone. "It's a great view of the ocean you have."

"What do you want?" Garrick growled.

Eros chuckled and glanced over his shoulder, dark blue eyes boring into him. "I have some information about your brother, Tyson. I think you'll find it very interesting."

The hairs on the back of Garrick's neck rose and he scented the air, taking in the aromas of the room. The one smell he expected wasn't there. Eros was telling the truth, or what the god of desire believed to be the truth. "Say what you came here for and leave. I'm busy."

Eros chuckled as he sat in Garrick's office chair. "Sophia's child is alive."

Garrick's heart stopped for a brief moment. His dragon growled and nudged him to ask where she was so they could bring her home. "Where is she?"

The god smiled. "I do not know."

Garrick fisted his hands. "Why are you wasting my time?"

Holding up a hand, Eros rolled his eyes. "The woman is not your daughter, as Sophia wanted you to believe."

Enough with the riddle crap. "Eros, I'm out of patience."

"She is Tyson's daughter. It seems she played both of you."

Fiery rage filled him. The child *was* his. "You lie."

The god raised a brow. "You need to tread lightly before you accuse a god. There are very few of us who give a shit about the Sons of War."

Screw that. He'd be damned if Ty would take another thing from him. However, Garrick wasn't stupid. He could play nice until he got what he wanted. "How do you know for sure?"

"I overheard your brother tell Ashlynn. Because he refused to join a triad with you and Sophia, the storm daemon tricked him into getting her pregnant before she went to you to complete the bond."

Not possible. He'd have known, wouldn't he? Ty would had told him. Or not. Yet another betrayal from his brothers. "I don't believe Ty's side of the story. He was jealous of my mating. They all were."

"One way to get back at Tyson would be to take his daughter or his mate."

Casting a narrow-eyed glare at Eros, Garrick asked, "What's in it for you?"

A wickedly evil grin formed on the god's face. "Revenge for the death of my Elizabeth."

Ty PACED the living room of his beach house while his brothers watched via Skype. Ash sat on the sofa waiting for someone to say something. Moments ago, he'd told Markus, Seth, and Drake about his captivity and lack of memory. Oh, and the real reason why Ash was with him.

After a long, painful silence, Markus spoke. "Gwen and I will search for a weaver. In the meantime, you need to try to remember what happened. Even the smallest clues can be helpful."

Nodding, Ty stopped pacing and rubbed his eyes under the shades. "I'll try."

The name Nik kept turning around in his mind and for the life of him he couldn't remember ever knowing anyone by the name. At least he hadn't remembered coming in contact with a Nik in the five centuries he'd been on earth.

Then there was Ash. The female captivated his dragon. The damn beast paced under his skin, wanting to feel her soft, creamy skin. To drown in her strawberry scent.

Giving the female his back as well as the others in the room with him, he met Markus's heavy stare in the monitor and snarled. Of course his brother watched him. Markus was more like Ares than the rest of them, meaning the male always watched, listened, and plotted their next move.

"Six days. I should just have Ash take me now, but the female is too damn stubborn. Do you know anyone by the name of Nik?"

Markus raked a hand through his hair. "I agree with Ash. You will remain with us for as long as we have. We will find the proof. As far as Nik…I'm not sure. We do have a brother named Nikolas. However, the last I heard, he moved around too much for Ares to keep track of him."

Ty stilled, his mind racing through possibilities. When they were created, there were thousands of warriors who'd fought in the war between the gods and their earth-bound children. All but about a dozen of them died, only six stayed in Olympus.

He never bothered to get to know any except Markus and Seth. For some reason Ty felt a deeper connection with them, like he was meant to stay with them. Now it all made sense. He was meant to serve a purpose in protecting not only earth, but Olympus as well.

"Do you think it's possible he is being held by

Garrick?" Why else would he be in the same room as Ty during his torture?

Markus sat back in his chair, brows drawn together as if in deep in thought. "It is possible. It's also possible he's there by choice."

Great. That's all they needed, two Sons of War working together. "Like he is on Garrick's side? No, that doesn't fit my flashback. The male who tried to talk to me was locked in a cage."

Ash stepped forward. "Are you sure?"

Ty shrugged. "Maybe sixty-five percent? The voice came from behind me." The dull ache returned in his temples as he tried to remember. Shoving the pain away, he focused until what he searched for surfaced. Then everything faded. It was like the spell Garrick placed on him didn't allow anything else to be revealed. "I heard chains as he spoke."

Ash paced the floor. "Garrick moved his prisoners around periodically. The locations were something he never shared with me. At the time, I didn't press or nose around because I didn't think he'd actually capture a dragon and be able to hold him."

Ty grunted and folded his arms as he leaned against the wall. "We know better now."

With a quick jerk of her head, she glared at him with narrowed eyes. Just as quick, her lips dipped into a frown and she averted her gaze. "I should have stayed longer, learned more about his operations."

Without another word, she stormed out the front

door. Ty pushed off the wall to follow her, but Markus cleared his throat. "You need to reconsider coming home. Together we can figure this shit out."

Instead of answering his brother, Ty shut off the computer and chased down his female.

He found her sitting in the sand several feet from the beach house, her back to him. When he reached her, he sat down beside her. "The past can't be changed. All we can do is move forward."

"I was sent to build a case, to find out the truth about Elizabeth's death. I got nothing from Garrick but anger, jealousy, and hatred. It was draining to be around. I should have been stronger." The sickly, sour scent of her anger drifted around him.

"You're not mad at yourself, so stop acting like it. Point the anger at the right person."

Her lips pressed together in a thin line as she studied him for a long moment. Finally, she spoke. "And who you are pissed off at?"

He shrugged, stretched his legs out and leaned back on his elbows. "Garrick, Sophia, Elizabeth…myself."

"Hypocrite."

He laughed while his dragon growled. "Ditto."

A small smile lifted the corners of her lips as she turned to gaze out over the ocean. They sat in silence for a while before she spoke again. "I never slept with Garrick." She'd drawn her knees to her chest and wrapped her arms around them. Sensing she wasn't finished, he remained silent and let her continue. "I've only been with one other man."

His dragon clawed at him from within and growled, wanting to get closer to her. Rising up on one arm, he gently took her chin and turned her face to his. "Why are you telling me this?"

"I'm not sure. I just didn't want you to think I…"

Not giving her time to finish her statement, her cupped her cheek and pressed his lips to hers. The gentle caress was unlike anything he'd experience. It was more personal than the kisses they'd shared before. She moaned, leaned into him and opened, inviting him in.

Sinking his fingers into her thick, silky hair, he tugged her closer. He slid his tongue inside her mouth, tangling with hers. Heat rolled through him while his dragon surfaced a little more. He pulled back, breaking the kiss, and held her desire filled gaze. She was beautiful and for the first time, he noticed the light dusting of freckles scattered across her nose.

Leaning in, he kissed the tip of her nose. "We'll figure this out. You are a strong female…with a pure heart."

She sagged into him as if his words chased her doubts away. His heart swelled and his dragon puffed out his chest in pride for making their female feel better.

Their female.

Realization settled in. The man wanted her as well.

Yet he couldn't have her. She was a goddess and he was under a death sentence. No, he wouldn't put her through a mating only to lose him.

He stood and offered her his hand. "Come, let's get some rest. Tomorrow, we travel to Maine."

CHAPTER SEVEN

The ocean was calm in the crisp early morning. Small waves broke on shore reaching out and kissing Ash's bare feet. The peach glow of the sunrise filled the sky. Closing her eyes, she sent out a call to her mother.

"Artemis, goddess of the hunt, I summon you."

A few moments later the goddess materialized beside her. "This is lovely."

Ash didn't answer. The scenery was indeed beautiful, but the report she had to give her mother was not. Delaying it would only piss off her mother, so Ash spoke her mind. "He didn't do it."

"Do you have proof?"

"No. He has no memories of the time he was held captive. Elle had another vision of the past."

Artemis sighed. "A painting will not please Eros's search for vengeance."

Fury boiled in her veins. "Nothing is going to please him. He paid Ty a visit and threatened Amissa's life. Did you know that?"

Turning her body, Ash stared into her mother's green eyes and crossed her arms. Artemis held her gaze, then let out a sigh. "No, I didn't."

"It was yesterday, at my townhouse."

Her mother's temples flexed and her eyes narrowed. "Then he's been watching you."

"Why me?"

"To lead him to Ty." Pausing, Artemis glanced back over the ocean. "Cyrus will protect Amissa, but keep her close anyway. There will be more eyes watching. You'll have to find evidence and bring your case to Zeus."

Heart sinking, Ash dropped her shoulders. Zeus disliked the dragons as much, if not more than Eros. However, Ash was not a quitter. She'd fine a way to save her dragon. Even if it meant sacrificing her own freedom.

Artemis touched her chin, drawing Ash's attention back to her. "You've fallen in love."

Stepping back, Ash shook her head, but it was no use. Her mother could always see through her. "Even if he did do it, it was justified. Elizabeth let desire consume her."

"You have to find the proof no matter how ugly it may turn out."

"I know."

Her mother's gaze darted to the side. "Your dragon is here."

Smiling, Ash leaned in and kissed the goddess's cheek. "I will find what I need."

Artemis squeezed her hand, then dematerialized. Taking a deep breath, she turned back to the sea and waited for Ty to approach.

When he came to a stop beside her and didn't say anything for several moments, she glanced up. He stood still as a rock, his spine straight and his gaze fixed on the ocean. Like the warrior and fierce predator he was made to be.

Turning her gaze back to the waves, she waited for him to speak. Her ability to connect to his dragon told her he didn't seek her out because he was lonely. Something bothered him and she guessed it was the flashback he had a few hours ago.

"I don't remember Nik."

She turned to face him then, drawing her brows together. "Why does that bother you so?"

"Because he knew me, called me by my birth name."

"I see. Garrick could had took him from your memories as well to hide the fact he held the dragon."

He let out a low growl. "How much access did you have to Garrick's prisoners?"

"None. He didn't trust me with that information."

"I heard others speak the name Nik a few times, but no one ever mentioned he was a dragon."

Ash searched her memories of the time she spent with Garrick and came up empty. "He didn't keep many captives, at least not at the places I've been to. The descendants either worked with him or died."

"Bastard."

"I agree. Garrick had no use to daemons unless they worked with him. He doesn't have the power to control them or capture them." She paused, then a thought came to mind. "What about the Sons of War who left Olympus after the war?"

"What about them?"

"How many were there? Could Garrick find any of them?"

Ty shrugged. "There were thousands of us. Only a dozen or so survived the war. We weren't granted immortality until after we won the war."

She faced him and raised her arm to touch his cheek, but he stepped back. The thought of letting him draw away came to mind a brief moment before she shoved it aside and stepped forward. Ty wasn't going to push her out, not since she'd had a taste of him.

"I'm not like Elizabeth. I'm not ruled by my desires." Well, at least not the power of desire. Ash rose on her toes and brushed her lips against his. "I'm ruled by the hunt. If you run from me, I'll give chase."

Through the dark shades, she saw the red glow of his eyes as he released a low growl and snaked an arm around her waist. With a quick jerk, he meshed their bodies together. She groaned at the feel of his hard body pressed into hers. But she didn't have time to respond before he sank one hand in her hair and pulled, forcing her head back.

A moment later his mouth claimed hers and his tongue thrust inside. At the same time one of his large, hard thighs slid between hers. She sucked on his tongue as she moved against his leg, sending slivers of desires through her.

With a tug of her hair, he broke the kiss. Their chests rose and fell in unison, indicating their bodies shared the same need. After a moment, Ty said roughly, "What spell have you cast over me?"

Her heart ached at the hint of distrust in his tone. However, she could never let him see the reaction. *Ever.* "I told you before, I will never use my powers against you. Have you felt me invade your mind or try to touch your dragon?" Okay, so she wasn't so successful in keeping her annoyance from her words. But, whatever.

One corner of his sensual mouth lifted in a half-grin. "That's not what I meant, goddess." He lowered his head so she felt his warm breath against her neck. She shivered. When he bit down on her earlobe, a bolt of hot desire hit her, dampening her panties. "I'm not mating material. I bite, hard."

The words, spoken on a deep, rough growl, made her want to give him anything he asked of her. "I'm fully aware of your bite."

Suddenly, his head snapped up and he scented the air. The hairs on the back of her neck stood on end right before she caught the scent of smoke. *Shit. Not good.* Before she could speak, Ty dematerialized, leaving her to stagger back a step.

Ash's next thought was Amissa. Dread crawled over her skin like a million ants, souring her stomach and pissing her the fuck off.

Teleporting to a few feet from the beach house, Ash conjured her bow and arrows and charged into the burning home. Just as she reached the door, Ty stepped into the entryway holding an unconscious Amissa in his arms. His rage washed over Ash like a tidal wave crashing over the coast. In the next instant, he closed the few feet between them and handed his daughter to her. "Take her to the mansion."

Ash took the female from Ty. When he turned to go back inside the house, Ash asked, "What are you doing?"

Without looking at her, he bit out, "I have to get Cyrus. Now do as I ask, Ashlynn."

A crackle of hot wood followed by a burst of flame made her step off the porch. With a curse, Ash held Amissa a little tighter and teleported to the dragons' mansion in Maine.

CHAPTER EIGHT

"You're one heavy son of a bitch."

Ty tried to keep his words playful, but worry for his friend overpowered his attempts. He'd found Cyrus face down in the hallway, bleeding from a deep gash across his chest. Thank the gods, his heart wasn't pierced.

"Yeah," Cyrus wheezed, then coughed before continuing. "You're a bastard."

A laugh burst from Ty's lips as he carried the larger male into the foyer of the mansion. "Fair enough."

A moment later, Maxwell, the house butler, appeared and placed his shoulder under Cyrus's other arm, taking some of the male's weight from Ty. "Ariel is preparing a room in the west wing."

Ty nodded as they made their way up stairs to the west side of the mansion. Once he'd gotten Cyrus into bed, Ariel—one of two nymphs living with them—went to work on the male's wound, applying a healing salve and softly chanting. Relief filled Ty when Cyrus relaxed and drifted to sleep.

He left the room to follow the connection he'd felt as soon as he entered the house to his daughter. They'd placed her in the room adjacent to Cyrus's. When he reached the door, he stopped short of the entrance at the sound of Ash's voice. "Your father only wants you to be safe."

There was a long silence before Amissa spoke. "You're in love with him."

Ty's heart stopped beating for several moments, and his body went still as he waited for Ash's response. "He's not the type of male to love."

He heard the rustle of sheets as if Amissa repositioned herself on the bed. "He has feelings for you."

"You don't know that."

"Yes, I do. I see the way he looks at you. The energy when you are together is intense."

Ty took a step away from the door. He'd never been able to shield his true feelings from his daughter, even in the short time he'd known her, so he didn't try. Never had he thought it would be used against him. Hearing her speak the words out loud and to Ash of all people was like a physical slap into reality.

He should walk away, find Markus and Zavier to start the hunt for the weaver. Yet, he couldn't make his body turn toward the stairs. Instead, he stepped into the bedroom. His gaze locked with Ash's the moment he did. She narrowed her eyes before facing the window again.

"I wondered how long you'd stand out in the hall." Her words were cooler than when she'd spoken to Amissa. He expected no less. Actually, he realized for the first time, it was the same tone he used on her. No, not the same. His words were harsher, driving a wedge between them because he wanted nothing to do with her. Or at least the man tried to tell the dragon. The beast would have none of it, however.

Ashlynn was his fated mate.

And she was here to bring him to the gods for punishment for his crimes. The Fates truly were bitches to give him his mate only to leave him unable to have her.

With a low growl, he moved to sit on the edge of the bed. Amissa looked well, but he could sense her pain. "What happened?"

His daughter forced a smile and took his hand. "Imperials broke down the door and attacked us. It happened so fast and there was so many of them." Her eyes went round as if panic started to settle in. "Cyrus. They stabbed him!"

Ty gathered her hands in his and kissed her knuckles. "He's fine. Ariel, one of Aphrodite's nymphs, is with him."

A frown formed in her features. "A female?"

Hiding a smile, he shook his head. "She is trained in healing."

She studied him for a moment, then relaxed. "You trust her?"

He started to say no, but it would be a lie. Sure, he growled at the nymphs, but only because they seemed to be a little too nosey. Their kind, nurturing personalities made them care too much about what happened to him. No matter how much he wanted to keep the details to himself, they knew. He blamed Aphrodite for that. The goddess most likely told them of his captivity. After all, nothing was secret from the gods. "Yes, I trust her and her sister Thea."

"Yet, you don't trust your own mate."

Ash made a noise in her throat before she stormed out of the room. *Shit.* How the hell did everything get fucked up? He stared into his daughter's gaze, not knowing how to answer. Then again it really wasn't a question.

Amissa sighed. "Go after her. I need to rest."

"It's complicated."

"I know why she's here. I also know she believes she can save you from the death sentence Eros has hanging over your head. You need to learn to trust her and work together to figure this shit out. I'm not going to let the gods take you from me any more than Ash will."

She tugged her hands free from his hold and rolled to her side. A hint of pride bloomed in his chest. Of course she knew why Ash was here as well as everything else going on. Amissa was telepathic and used her gift to get answers.

Leaning down, he pressed a kiss to her temple and whispered. "Prying into others' thoughts is rude."

She laughed. "Not if I'm protecting my father from heartache. And don't dare deny your feelings to me."

"Brat," he teased. "Get some sleep."

He rose and left the room and searched for Markus, fighting the urge to follow Ash's scent. If he went to her now, they'd end up naked and panting. Ty needed to focus on regaining his memory and finding a weaver. Maybe then he'll be able to prove Elizabeth was indeed lost to her desires and not the devoted goddess she made her father believe she was.

He didn't need the complications of a mate to distract him.

ASH WHIRLED, thrust her leg up and kicked out, nailing the large sandbag hanging in the back of the gym. The kick was hard enough the chain suspending the bag snapped and it dropped to the ground.

Damned dragon. Stupid-ass male.

He knew they were mates and chose to ignore it. She shouldn't be surprised, but it didn't mean it didn't hurt. And why? Because she dared to let hope enter her heart. Hope she'd save his life while healing his broken soul.

Footsteps from behind made her whirl around to face the intruder. Elle stopped half way across the gym on her way to her studio. Ash relaxed and straightened. "Sorry. I was blowing off some steam and you startled me."

Elle's gaze flicked to the punching bag on the floor, then back at Ash. "I see that." The female narrowed her eyes slightly as if studying Ash. After a few moments, Elle said, "Can I ask you an odd question?"

Curious, Ash nodded. What could it hurt? She didn't know much about the other woman other than she was the daughter of Nyx, goddess of night. Plus Ash could use a distraction. "Yes, as long as it's not offensive."

Elle's shoulder dropped and a faint smile lifted her lips, clearly sensing Ash's playfulness behind her words. "Can I paint you?"

Okay, Ash didn't see that coming. "Why? I mean, I think I'm flattered, but why me?"

Elle shrugged and started toward her studio, which was one half of a room she shared with Zavier. Distracted to her satisfaction, Ash followed the dark haired demi-goddess. "Do you paint live subjects often?"

Pausing at the door, Elle glanced back at her. "Not usually. I've only done two others."

The catch in her voice made Ash's heart skip a beat. A sad, but dark sensation shuttered over her skin. She feared she wouldn't like the answer, but she asked the question anyway. "Who were the other two?"

With a heavy sigh, Elle turned away and opened the door. "My parents, the night before they died."

Fuck. She had to ask. "I'm sorry…"

Elle shrugged and motioned to the love seat against the far wall. "Have a seat and be as comfortable as you'd like."

Ash did as the other woman asked and laid on her back with her knees over the arm to allow her legs to dangle. Watching Elle set up the canvas and easel, Ash couldn't help but wonder about her. "You and Gwen grew up together?"

A smile stretched the corners of Elle's lips. "We became instant friends in the third grade."

Warmth bloomed in Ash's heart, while at the same time loneliness settled in. She'd never had a friendship as strong as Gwen and Elle's. In fact, the only close relationship she had was with her mother. Artemis never let her out of her sight as a child.

With a slight sigh, Elle continued talking as she settled onto a stool in front of the canvas. "My parents died when I was sixteen. Gwen's parents took me in and treated me like their own daughter."

The longing welcomed sadness back in. Ash studied the other woman and without thinking about it, said, "I never knew my father."

Elle stilled and met her gaze. Her mouth dropped into a frown. "Your mother never told you?"

A humorless laugh burst from Ash. "Artemis? I love my mother more than anything, but she is a goddess in every sense of the word. The one time I asked about him, she said he was dead and it pained her to speak of him. I never asked again."

Picking up a pencil from the workbench, Elle started to sketch. "I sense you didn't let it go."

"No. I tried to search and ask around. But no one seemed to know or just didn't care who he was. It wasn't until I was given access to the archives when I was given to job to…well spy on the Sons of War." Ash stared up at the ceiling, feeling like a traitor for the admission.

"The gods have their reasons for sending you. From what I've learned in the short time of being here, they don't trust the dragons."

Ash turned her head to watch Elle. She was right. The gods had good reason not to trust the sons of Ares. Even the god of war wasn't well liked by the others.

After a long silence, Elle asked, "What did you find in the archives?"

Stunned, Ash considered not telling the woman. What would it hurt to tell her? *Nothing.* "I found a name of a god banished to earth to live as a mortal. It's usually the punishment for treason. Yet, his crimes were not noted."

"Why not?"

"Not sure. It could mean the oracle either didn't know, which is highly unlikely, or she was forbidden to record certain facts." Ash was betting on the latter. If

Zeus didn't want others to know something, he'd forbid the oracle from noting it.

Elle stopping drawing and studied Ash for a few moments. "What is it about the name stands out to you?"

Instinct, mainly. "The fact no one ever spoke of this god, not even in the human historical or mythological literatures. It was as if he never existed."

"Well, go find out who he is, then."

New purpose, or at least a new focus away from the mess of emotions surrounding Ty, filled her mind. She could search out this god while the dragons sought a weaver. It would give her the needed space away from Ty. A break for her to clear her mind and focus on how to save Ty's life while solving another mystery plaguing her thoughts since finding the file the oracle directed her to.

"Thanks, Elle. I think I'll do that."

CHAPTER NINE

"So how long have you kept Amissa a secret from us?"

Ty set his jaw at Markus's question. "She is my daughter and mine to protect."

Markus leaned forward from behind his desk and growled, "We are your brothers and her uncles. We *all* will protect her."

"She has a guardian." Ty sighed and laid his head against the back of the couch. "She was safer away from us. Plus I didn't know how you'd take it if you knew she was Sophia's daughter."

"Fuck, Ty."

Yeah, he failed to share who her mother was when he told his brothers about Amissa the day before. "It was a one-nighter before she mated with Garrick." He went on explaining his and Ash's theory on how Sophia wanted both and could only have one or the other.

Markus fell silent and Zavier took the moment to speak up. "The real problem here is Eros. We need to find a weaver to unlock Ty's memories so Ashlynn can present her case."

Seth glanced from Zavier to Ty, then to Markus. "I think Z's been keeping his own secrets."

Zavier grit his teeth and spoke through them. "Those secrets are not mine to share."

Ty snapped his head up and let out a growl so loud it rumbled the windows in the room. "Enough! Why the fuck are we arguing over this? I have a death sentence over my head for killing Eros's daughter. I doubt he'll even listen to whatever evidence we come up with anyway."

Markus cocked a brow. "He has to go through a trial."

Ty let out a bitter laugh. "Oh, he'll go through the trial and most likely twist everything Ash brings up."

"Then we have to be prepared when the time comes." Markus tapped his fingers on the desk, then added, "Gwen and I will leave in the morning to search for the weaver. Amissa and Cyrus are welcome to stay here."

Nodding, Ty said, "I know. I thought I was protecting her by keeping her existence a secret. Now Eros knows…"

Zavier cursed, drawing Ty's attention. "The imperials attacked her home."

Seth finished the thought. "Which means Garrick knows about her."

The same thought kept running through his mind. A number of possibilities ran inside his head. The top two being Garrick could have one of his weavers create a locator spell, but Ty wasn't sure how his brother would get ahold of anything personal to find Amissa. Unless he didn't need something from Amissa, but Ty. The second possibility would be Eros aiding Garrick in the search. The later seems more plausible since Eros would use whatever reason he could to get what he wanted.

"What could Garrick have that Eros wants?" Ty wondered out loud, not directing the question to any in particular.

Yet, Markus answered. "There is the divine dagger from Elle's painting."

Only Ty didn't remember seeing the dagger or Garrick with it. If he did have it, Ty doubted his brother would just hand it over to Eros or any of the gods. No, there had to be something else the dragon possessed valuable enough for Eros to desire.

"You know…" Seth began as he paced in front of the windows in the study. "Eros could just being using Gary to get at you. If he succeeded in capturing, or even killing, Amissa, it'd push you over the edge."

Drake growled. "Proving to the gods you are indeed insane. Amissa stays here."

If Garrick or anyone else touched Amissa, there would be no holding the dragon back. The world would definitely see what it truly meant to deal with an insane dragon.

Suddenly, the room around him dissolved and he found himself standing in the cold, too-clean room of his captivity. When his vision cleared, he saw himself strapped to a table in the middle of the room. Scanning his surroundings, he noted several large cages around the outer edge of room. A few of them had prisoners in them, but he couldn't get a clear visual on them.

The door opened and Elizabeth entered holding an amber jar in one hand and gloves and a dropper in the other. As she approached the table, he thrashed and growled at her, trying to get a hold of her, but the chains binding him made movement nearly impossible.

"So strong, yet so weak," she purred as she set the items she carried on the tray next to the table.

Fury and buried pain flooded his senses as he watched her remove the lid and dip the dropper inside. Memories of the agony those drops caused him surfaced. With a roar, he leapt into the air toward her, but instead of tackling her to the ground and stopping history, he went right through her. Like he wasn't really there. But he was there. He could see everything in the room.

A scream cut through the room, shaking the cabinets and pictures on the walls. Pain exploded in his head and his right eye as if he was being tortured all over again.

"Ty!"

He heard his name, but couldn't make his brain work enough to lock onto the voice.

"Ty."

The second voice was different, more commanding, yet softer. Markus. The voice belonged to his brother. Slowly the pain eased and he opened his eyes. The sudden bright light of the study stung his eyes, telling him someone—maybe him—removed his shades.

Seth's face came into view, blocking the light. "Dude, you scared the shit out of us."

Scowling, Ty realized he was flat on his back on the study floor. His brothers hovered around him like he was an injured hatchling. He pushed to his feet and when he briefly lost his balance, Markus reached out. Shrugging out of his reach, Ty shook off the wave of dizziness and left the study. There was only one person he wanted to have touch him.

He needed to find his mate.

CHAPTER TEN

Ash materialized behind an automotive shop in a small mountain town in Georgia. Her nerves were like live electrical wires, making her stomach twist in knots. Taking a deep breath, she forced her legs to move. The man who owned the shop might not be her father. She could be wasting her time with silly childhood hope.

His name was Evan Martin.

It didn't sound much like a Greek god's name. Then again, it was an alias he used to live among humans. His real name was Evangelos, according to her research. Besides, the oracle was never wrong.

Rounding the corner to the front of the garage, she cloaked herself with an invisibility spell her mother taught her when she was a teen. She wasn't ready to face the man. First she had to be sure he was her father.

Evan made an appearance at one of the bay openings. Ash's heart stilled for a brief moment as she stared at him. His black hair brushed the tops of his shoulders, but when he lifted his gaze in her direction, he stole her breath. His eyes were identical to her own.

With a single thought, she teleported back to her hotel room in the nearby town, Dahlonega, and sat on the edge of the bed, her hand over her mouth. A single tear rolled down her cheek. *Okay, Ash, calm down and think.*

Rising to her feet, she left the room to head down to the restaurant connected to the hotel. She needed to think, but didn't feel like being alone. A public place would help, she hoped. So many questions whirled in her mind. Did he know he had a daughter? Did he even want one?

She shouldn't have come. Damn, she was such a chicken.

Ten minutes after taking her seat, the all too familiar presence of a dragon drifted into her awareness. A moment later, Ty sat in the chair across the small round table from her, his lips set in a thin, firm line. Ash sipped her herbal tea and sat back in her chair.

"I expected you sooner," she said after lowering her cup.

He leaned forward and growled, "Can we go somewhere more private?"

Well, there was a first. He'd actually asked. "I came here to think."

After she set her cup down, he reached and gripped her wrist and tugged her closer. "I will not ask again."

Yep, he was pissed. Movement behind him caught her eye. The waitress slowly advanced toward them, concern making her brows dip. Ash smiled wide and leaned into Ty, nipping his bottom lip. A low growl rumbled from his throat. His dragon was so close to the surface, she felt him reach out to her without the use of her empathy.

When the waitress stopped at their table, Ash held Ty's gaze as she spoke to the woman. "Can you have my breakfast sent to my room?"

After a brief pause, the waitress answered. "Of course, miss."

Once the server walked away, Ty stood, still holding onto Ash's wrist. She jerked her arm from his grasp and left the restaurant to head to her room. To her surprise, Ty was quiet along the way. However, she could feel his gaze behind those shades boring into her back.

After entering her room, she turned to face him, arms crossed. Ty let the door slam behind him as he crossed the short distance between them. Holding out a hand, she stopped him at arm's length. He leaned forward so her palm flattened to his chest. Heat seeped into her flesh and spread up her arm. "What is your problem?"

He growled and removed his shades. His left eye, the good one, shifted to match the right eye so the dragon looked out both of them. Ash raised her brows. Did he seriously think he could intimidate her?

After a brief moment, he said, "I looked for you and you weren't there."

"I needed my space. Besides, it's not like you care anyway."

He moved too fast for her to track, which was pretty damned fast. Within a breath of time, he had her back pressed to his front and one large arm locked around her chest. "I care too damn much. My dragon won't allow anything less. I crave you every second of the day. When you weren't in the mansion, I had no choice but to track you down."

His admission cut through her, making her muscles tense up. The dragon might want her, but the man did not. Just like pouring alcohol into an open wound. Why was she so damn weak when it came to him? Pushing the feeling of rejection away, she twisted out of his hold and faced him. Surprise made his eyes grow round for a brief moment, then his lips curled into a sensual, hungry smile.

Her heartbeat increased and she stepped back as he stalked toward her. Desire, lust, and need reached out and swirled around her, amplifying her own sexual hunger. Still she continued to back away from him for the pure thrill of being chased and hunted by him.

The backs of her legs hit the mattress, throwing her off balance so she fell onto the bed. Ty followed, caging her with his arms. Gazes still locked, he claimed her mouth in a fiery need, igniting her from the inside out.

Unable to stand it anymore, she cupped the back of his head and kissed him. She thrust her tongue inside, meeting his. He moaned and wrapped an arm around her to lift her further up on the bed.

Her clothes vanished from her body as if he willed it to be. As one of Ares's sons, Ty possessed the powers equal to the gods. His dragon half provided him, as well as his brothers, strength and primal instincts that amplified those powers.

Ty broke the kiss and trailed his lips down her throat to her collarbone and further until he took a nipple into his mouth. Tingles of electrical currents raced through her and straight to her core. Her flesh grew more and more sensitive with each brush of his tongue over her nipple.

When he abandoned her breast, she whimpered, then sucked in a hiss as his mouth covered her pussy. His tongue teased her clit, making her come instantly. Threading her fingers through his hair, she gripped the strands, rotated her hips and rode the wave of bliss.

He slid two fingers inside her and a rush of hot, bone-shattering sensation surged in her veins. An orgasm ripped through a moment later, making her scream out in pleasure.

When the last shudder rocked through her, Ty gave one last lap of his tongue and crawled up her body. She waited until he hovered above her, then in a swift jerk of her legs, she flipped them so she straddled his still clothed body. Leaning down, she bit his earlobe, drawing a growl from him. "You're still dressed."

"Then do something about it."

With the same divine magic he'd used, she willed his clothes away, removing the cotton and denim barrier from between them. He didn't take his gaze from hers as she gripped his cock in her hand and guided him inside her. She slowed to allow her body to adjust to his thick cock. After all, this was the second man she'd had sex with.

Ty tightened his grip on her hips and hissed as she rotated her hips against him. He followed suit, increasing the tempo and the pleasure racing through her. Her control slipped and her senses opened, allowing his dragon inside her mind. The walls she kept up to keep her empathy at bay crashed. His pleasure became hers and hers, his.

Suddenly, he rolled them over and studied her from above. "What happened?"

Fear she just broke the trust she'd worked so hard to gain filled her. "I lost control...I didn't mean to."

He drew his brows together, then kissed her with a passion she'd never felt from him before. "Don't ever apologize to me for being who you are."

"I promised you..."

He bit down on her bottom lip, cutting her off. "That was shared pleasure. And very hot."

Another wave of intense pleasure washed over them as he thrust inside her. She fisted the sheets and just let go, loving the way she connected with both the man and the dragon's spirit within him. Pleasure built higher with each thrust until they screamed in release.

CHAPTER ELEVEN

In his long life, he'd never been the kind of male to cuddle with anyone. Yet, with Ash he want to hold her, protect her, and give her what she desired. The realization slammed in him as he lied there in the hotel bed, her head on his chest and her red wavy hair draped over them.

Holding a one-inch wide curl between his fingers, he studied the different shades of red mingled among the strands and did something he swore he'd never do again. He lowered the walls around his heart. "I'm sure I'll never be the male I once was. You know, before Elizabeth's torture."

Ash raised her head to gaze into his eyes, tugging the curl out of his grasp. With a finger, she traced the scars over his right brow. "I like you the way you are. Damaged and feral. Who else could handle me?"

His lips twitched. "Damaged and feral?"

She nibbled her bottom lip, making her look slightly vulnerable. Damn if he didn't want to be the one biting that lip. "Yep." Dipping her head, she caught his lower lip in her teeth, then said, "I like my men a little wild."

Within quick efficiency, he flipped her to her back and pinned her to the mattress with his body. "I can't get enough of you."

Her emerald eyes darkened a few shades. "What are you saying?"

A growl escaped him before he could rein it in. "You know what I mean."

"Say it, Ty. I want to hear it from you."

He studied her for several moments before forcing the words out. "You're my mate."

Her reaction wasn't what he expected. He'd guessed she already knew they were mates before he said it, but he didn't expect her to appear relieved he admitted it. *Damn female.* Before he could roll off her and make his escape like a coward, she cupped his face between her hands and gave him a quick kiss.

"I will do everything I can to clear you name. Eros will not get away with executing you for something his daughter provoked."

Searching her green gaze, he saw only truth. She believed what she said, that she could save his life. "What if I'm not worth saving? I'm not sure what the weaver will unlock."

She narrowed her eyes. "You have to believe with me and trust in me. I can't let you go."

His heart ached. The undertone of her words cut deep and was a little too close to a commitment. Yet, for once he didn't want to run. He wanted to believe. "That is a big request to make."

"I know. I'll wait as long as it takes."

Mischief and stubbornness sparked in her gaze, so he decided to change the subject. They would deal with the mating thing later. Like after his life was spared. "Why are you here?"

All the humor faded from her face and she averted her gaze. She remained silent for several long moments. His patience grew thin. When he let a low growl rumble from his chest, she snapped her gaze back to his. Annoyance lit up her emerald eyes, but there was an undercurrent of sadness hidden in the depths.

The sadness made his dragon long to hold her, protect her. Gently, he caressed her cheek with the backs of his fingers. "Tell me, please."

"I found my father."

He jerked his head back, surprised. Parents weren't the kind of thing Ty or his brothers thought about. Their existence just was. The only true parent they had— Ares's son, Drakon Ismenios—died before they were created. All their lives, they'd called Ares father and never gave a thought otherwise. Times like this Ty had to remember that others had parents—a mother and father.

Of course Ash had a father.

"Why haven't you mentioned him? Was he missing?"

She pressed her palms against his chest and shoved. Rolling to his side, he allowed her to sit up. All the while concern rippled through him, making him feel uneasy and unsure for the first time since Elizabeth.

Ash glanced at him from over her shoulder. "My mother always told me my father was mortal and he died. Even as a child, I knew the loss of him pained her, so I never brought it up."

"But something changed?"

Nodding, she rose and walked bathroom where she slipped a black silk robe on. "When I was told to spy on the Sons of War, the oracle pointed me to a group of archives to aid in my research." She paused and faced him, holding his gaze as she continued. "There was a ledger that didn't belong. When I asked her about it, she just rambled on about everything is as it should be."

Ty rolled to his back and placed his hands behind his head. "Oracles don't make mistakes. Do you think she placed the ledger there for you to find?"

"Yes. The ledger was of a god named Evangelos, minor god of messengers."

Turning his head, he met her gaze. "And?"

Leaning against the bathroom doorframe, Ash rolled the tie to the robe between her fingers. "He was cursed to live on earth as a mortal. There was a section missing from his journal, so I don't know his crime."

He studied her for a long moment, waiting for her to

continue. When she remained silent, he asked, "What are you not saying?"

"Mother said he was dead. What bothers me about the whole thing is she believes it. She is deeply saddened by the mention of him, so I've never brought it up."

"Do you think she's being truthful about his death?"

Ash raised her gaze to his, the annoyed fire lighting up the green of her eyes. "She's a goddess. If he meant nothing to her, she'd just tell me so. Ditto if he used or hurt her in any way. No, she believes he is dead. I'm sure of it."

He swung his legs over the side of the bed, sitting up at the same time. "Get dressed."

"What? Why?"

"We're going to pay dear daddy a visit."

ASH STARED at Ty as he willed on only a pair of jeans. The dragon had serious control issues, barking out commands like she was supposed to jump to attention. "I can't."

He raised a brow. "Yes, you can."

She pushed off the doorframe and strode toward him. "You're a bossy ass."

His sensual mouth lifted at the corners, but there was pure mischief in his gaze. When she walked by him instead of stopping in front him, he snaked one arm around her waist, jerking her back into his front. He pressed his lips to her neck, then growled, "Don't push me, female."

Hot shivers of desire skittered over her skin and rushed through her veins. She wanted to twist around and push him back on the bed, rip his jeans from him, and fuck him like he did her earlier. Memories of the pleasure he gave her multiple times made her moan.

He inhaled and tightened his hold. "On second thought, push. I'm going to enjoy bringing you to submission."

A smile tugged at her lips. "Only in the bedroom, *drakon.*"

Chuckling, he nipped at her earlobe. "Get dressed, goddess."

He let her go abruptly and she had to reach out for the dresser to catch her balance. The desire and need he raised within her was dizzying.

Damned dragon.

Less than five minutes later, they materialized a few feet from the garage where Evangelos worked. Ash watched for movement inside the bays. "He goes by the name of Evan Martin."

Ty grunted next to her, much too close for her heightened senses. "Common name. Almost perfect for hiding amongst humans."

Yeah, she'd thought the same thing. But was it by her father's choice or the god who cursed him? Taking a deep breath, she pushed forward. "Let's get this over with."

When they entered the first bay of the garage, she spied Evan with his head under the open hood of a car. As if sensing her, he jerked to a stand and glared at her.

"You." He stalked toward her, anger in his green eyes.

She backed up, unsure what to expect. Then he suddenly grabbed her by the throat. Ty moved in behind him, but Ash shook her head hoping he would let her handle it. To her relief, Ty stopped, but fixed a narrowed eye on Evan as if not liking the other man's hands on her. Well, she couldn't blame him. She was a little annoyed with the situation too.

Focusing on Evan, she said softly, "You have me mixed up with some else."

"I think not, goddess."

She sighed. At times like these, she didn't like looking like her mother. At least she knew he was her father. "Let me go so we can go inside and talk. We'll draw a crowd out here."

He narrowed his eyes, a mixture of pain and anger making them darken. "I'll let you go and kick you out of my business. You're not welcome here."

Her heart ached as rejection started to settle in. Pushing it way, she dropped the news on him she'd hoped to break to him gently. "I'm not Artemis. I'm her daughter…and yours."

He paused and searched her eyes. Of course he

wouldn't believe her. His gaze flicked to his right shoulder. "Who's the dragon?"

"My mate."

Releasing her, Evan stepped back from both of them. "I have no daughter. Tell the gods their tricks no longer work to taunt me. Leave now, before I call the police."

He turned and walked into the small office on the far side of the garage. Ash's nose tingled and her vision blurred as fat tears filled her eyes and rolled down her cheeks. Ty stepped in close and hugged her to his chest. Then he teleported them out of there.

CHAPTER TWELVE

Gwen drummed her fingers on the desk in the hotel room she and Markus checked into an hour ago. They gotten the first lead on a weaver. "Why do they hide?"

Markus massaged her shoulders gently. "Because, love, they use to be hunted by daemons for their powers. The few left do everything they can to hide their true natures."

"And that's why I'm perfect for locating them," she said dryly.

Leaning down, he kissed her cheek and then her neck. Warmth spread through her, making her smile. Gods, she loved him with every fiber of her being. They were a mated pair, bonded to each other—soul, mind, and body. His strength was hers and hers, his.

Gwen would have it no other way.

Markus was hers, as was his dragon.

His low growl vibrated against her skin. "Your desires drive me crazy."

She pressed her thighs together as his need filtered down the mating bond. All of the sudden, he was gone. Turning her head, she found him looking through the peephole in the door. A ting of fear made her heart rate spike a little.

Closing her eyes, she breathed in and out slowly to calm the panic that still haunted her. After all, watching her father die in front of her eyes by a fire breathing dragon and spending fourteen years running from the dragon kind of made her edgy. Okay, so she was a little more than edgy. More like a pathetic mess who suffered from panic attacks at every loud noise.

"Gwen?" Markus's concerned, low tone broke her from her thoughts.

She waved her hand at him over her shoulder. "I'm fine."

The door clicked open and the oddest sensation circled her, kissing her bare arms. Turning toward the now open door, she stared at the woman who walked into the room at Markus's encouragement.

Standing about five foot four with modest curves and long, curly, fiery red hair, the woman was pretty and glowed from inner magic. The glow was her magical signature, an aura. Gwen wasn't sure how she saw it. She was almost tempted to ask Markus if he saw the soft ice blue hue, which surrounded the woman.

"I'm Selene, the weaver you've been looking for."

Gwen blinked, then turned to Markus, who shrugged and closed the door. Focusing back on Selene, Gwen rose from her chair. "I'm sorry. I'm being rude. I didn't expect you to just show up."

Selene laughed softly, a beautiful and infectious child-like sound. "You and your dragon are drawing too much attention with your inquiries."

"What do you mean? We were discreet." Gwen glanced at Markus for some kind of reassurance. Of course, he didn't give it.

Selene sighed. "Most the people in town know what I am and are very aware some seek to harm me and anyone standing in their way."

"Oh."

Markus walked over to stand next to Gwen, his arms folded over his chest. "Will you help us?"

Holding a hand up, Selene shook her head. "Not so fast, dragon. You haven't told me what you want. Nothing comes free."

"We'll pay you for your time." Markus shot back with a low growl.

Selene glanced to Gwen. "Does he always growl?"

Nodding, Gwen tried to hide her smile. "Yes. We seek a weaver to help break a memory spell."

Tapping her chin with an index finger, Selene thought about it while studying the two of them. After a couple of moments, she asked, "Memory spells are tricky. Are you sure it is a spell?"

Gwen looked over at Markus, waiting for him to answer. He rolled his eyes at her, then turned to Selene. "Not a hundred percent. Will you come to Maine with us and help?"

Folding her arms over her chest, Selene glared at him. "I can't just up and leave. I have…responsibilities here."

Markus took a step, but Gwen reached out and closed her hand over his forearm, stopping him. Gwen offered her hand to Selene. "You know I'm the granddaughter of one of the Fates." When the woman nodded, Gwen continued, "Then you know I can't lie."

"You can twist your words to not be a lie, but to mean something else."

Gwen rolled her eyes. "Yes, but it takes too much effort. I find it a waste of my time. Time I don't have in this moment."

She tried to keep the annoyance out of her tone, but failed. Ty's life depended on unlocking his memories and discovering what really went on during his captivity. "Selene, please. We need your help, so please come with us. I give my word, you will not be harmed while at the mansion."

Shaking her head, Selene started to pace. Gwen could sense her unease and fear. Her own patience grew thinner with each passing moment. Eagerness to get the weaver to Ty flowed through her, setting her on edge. She wanted to grab the woman and teleport her back to

Maine. Or at least use force to get Selene to them help solve the mystery behind the gods' accusations so they could begin building their own case for Ty's judgment.

Releasing a heavy sigh, Gwen shook off the urges to do something completely out of character. She really didn't know what had gotten into her lately. It seemed her newfound powers made her more violent and protective...

She turned her gaze to Markus on the heels of that thought. Could she be?

Suddenly, the room seemed to grow warmer, then a wave of dizziness washed over her, making her stumble back to grip the back of the chair. Just as the dizziness faded, nausea rose and she rushed to the bathroom, slamming the door behind her as she ran to the toilet and heaved up her breakfast.

MARKUS STARED at the closed bathroom door, confused and stunned. *What the fuck just happened?* He strode to door and tapped on it. "Gwen?"

When she didn't answer, he yanked the door open and found her sitting on the floor with her forehead resting on the toilet seat. He tugged a hand towel from the towel bar and ran it under cold water before kneeling down beside his mate. "What is it?"

He didn't know how to care for someone who was

sick. He'd never had to deal with illness himself. Come to think of it, neither should Gwen. His heart hammered at the thought. What if someone poisoned her? He should had never brought her here, expose her to Garrick and his imperials.

"Gwen?" he pleaded softly.

She waved a hand and shook her head as she rose to her feet. Markus gripped her elbow when she swayed. "I'm fine, now."

"She is with child."

Markus whirled his gaze to Selene, standing in the doorway watching them. Reality hit him like a two-ton boulder to the chest. Disbelief clouded his thoughts for a brief moment. Then joy sparked in his heart at the thought of a child, along with fear and an overwhelming need to protect. His dragon paced within, wanting out to fly Gwen far away from everyone and everything.

Gwen sagged into him and wrapped her arms around his waist. "I was so worried for you and Ty, I ignored the signs."

He hugged her close and kissed the top of her head. "Me too, love."

Since he got smacked with a healthy dose of reality and clarity, he noticed the slight change in her scent. It wasn't like he hadn't noticed before. Gwen was an emotional and caring person. Her scent changed often as she continued to learn to control her panic attacks, which only came when she was out in public. Then there was her new powers.

Hell, it was like relearning everything about her.

Now they were going to be parents.

"We need to get you home." He scooped her up in his arms and carried her out of the bathroom, causing Selene to dart out of the way. "Aphrodite!"

A moment later the love goddess materialized next to him. "Must you shout?" She paused, then let out a small squeak. "Oh! Gwen's pregnant."

When the goddess reached for Gwen, Markus turned so she'd be out of reach. "She's ill."

Aphrodite propped her fist on her hips and tapped the toe of one pink heel she wore. Markus glanced at the tapping shoe, then up to the goddess face, and raised a brow. Annoyance flowed from her. "My granddaughter is not ill. She's pregnant. Morning sickness—I have no idea why they call it that—can come at any time of the day. And for the love of Zeus, put her down. She's not fragile."

Gwen wiggled in his arms, so he slowly set her on her feet. "Can she teleport home?"

"Yes. Thea will be able to help her through the pregnancy." Aphrodite smiled wildly until Selene cleared her throat behind them.

"Aphrodite, this is Selene, the weaver."

Beside him, Aphrodite froze and stared at the other female. Gwen noticed too and pushed past him to touch the goddess on the shoulder. "*Yaya*, what is it?"

The goddess blinked and smiled. "I'm sorry. There is something familiar about you."

Selene glanced to Gwen, then back to Aphrodite. "I'm not sure what you mean. I've lived in this town all my life."

Aphrodite shrugged and turned back to Markus. He studied her for a long moment. There was something she wasn't telling them. He didn't have time to read into it at the moment. Ty needed the weaver.

"Selene, please come with us. As Gwen said, no harm will come to you."

The weaver dropped her shoulders. "I have to go collect my things and my son."

"Your son?" he and Gwen asked at the same time.

Selene nodded. "He's fifteen months old."

Markus inhaled deeply, then released the breath in a rush. His patience wore thinner and thinner by the second. "What about his father?"

Sadness flowed from her and she hung her head. "He was killed by Imperials before Trenton was born."

Fuck.

No wonder the female was afraid and mistrusting. "I'll escort you to get your son. Aphrodite, take Gwen home."

Gwen narrowed her eyes at him, but before she could argue, he stepped closer to her, cupped her face, and kissed her. Pulling back, he met her heated, desire-filled gaze. His lips twitched. "Please, love, don't argue."

Aphrodite let out a soft laugh and linked her fingers

with her granddaughter's. "Come, dear. He will only get worse now that you are carrying his child."

With a heavy heart, he locked down control over his dragon to keep the beast contained while their mate dematerialized from their sight. Good gods, he was going to be a father.

CHAPTER THIRTEEN

Ash watched the fish swim around, carefree and happy, in the small pond in her mother's garden. For the first time, she wished she was with the fish and just as ignorant to how much people sucked.

She sensed her mother before she heard her. Not bothering to get up, she waited for her. They were close and Artemis always knew when Ash was upset. The goddess would come searching for her, just as Ash wanted.

A moment later, Artemis sat on the large boulder beside her. "Your heart is broken."

It was more than broken. *Try smashed.* Instead of answering, Ash shrugged, trying to find the right words to form the questions whirling in her mind. There was no gentle way to bring up the subject of her father, especially to a woman who seemed to be fine forgetting him.

"You shouldn't put yourself through this. Bring

Tyson in for judgment and be done with it. The pain will ease in time."

Ash jerked her gaze to her mother, annoyance bubbling up. "This isn't about Ty. In fact, I believe more than ever he couldn't ever kill Elizabeth."

Artemis's expression didn't change. It remained the cool, practiced, and perfect features of the goddess of the hunt. "Why?"

"Because he believed Elizabeth could have been his mate."

"That does throw a wrench into things, doesn't it? So why are you sad?"

Ash turned her attention back to the fish. "I found my father today."

"What? That's not possible. Your father died before you were born."

There was a tremble in her voice Ash hadn't heard before. Gazing back at her mother, she took her hands, which shook. Ash drew their linked hands to her chest. "Mama, look at me. I would never lie to you. Not about this. I believe you believed he died. But I saw him today. I saw my eyes in the face of an auburn haired, mocha-skinned man."

Artemis's bottom lip trembled. "How?"

"The oracle." Ash went on to tell her about the ledger and where she'd found him. "He thought I was you and was very angry."

The goddess frowned. "Did you tell him you were his daughter?"

Ash nodded. "Yes, but I didn't get a chance to say anything else before he kicked us out."

Artemis tugged her hands free and stood. "Evangelos and I were in love. We kept it a secret, unsure how others would react. He was only half-god. His mother was a siren. Many feared him and thought he was unworthy to live in Olympus. When Zeus found out about our affair, he was furious. Then Evan left. A few days later, Zeus came to me and told me he died."

Tears streamed down Artemis's face. Ash threw her arms around her mother and squeezed. "Oh, *mitera*. I'm so sorry."

Artemis pulled back out of the hug and framed Ash's face in her hands. "I have you. My beautiful daughter who is so much like her father."

A weak smile lifted Ash's lips and she hugged her mother again. *There has got to be a way to bring them back together and figure out why he was banned to earth.* No matter how long it took, she would find out.

Ty LET OUT A LOW GROWL. "Female, what did I tell about being in my room?"

Ash faced him, brows raised and a smile on her face. "If I got my scent in your space, you'd fuck me until I scream."

Damn. His cock jerked to attention, pressing painfully against the zipper of his jeans. With three quick strides, he stood in front her. He wrapped an arm tightly around her waist, holding her against his body.

Then he saw it. Sadness stole the fire from her eyes, though she tried hard to hide it. "What happened?"

She let out a soft sigh and laid her head against his chest while she hugged him closer. Ty loosened his hold and just held her, not knowing what to do. His strong, stubborn hunter was hurting, and he didn't have a clue on how to fix it.

After several long moments, she finally spoke. "They were in love. Zeus cursed Evangelos and told *mitera* he died."

Anger heated his blood. The gods fought with each other about as much as the humans, jealousy and power being the main causes of strife. He had no doubt both were involved in tearing Ash's parents apart.

For Ash to call Artemis mother to him told him just how much it pained her. Usually she called the goddess of the hunt by her name, and he'd bet only called her *ma* or *mitera* in private—the address common among the gods and their children.

With his index finger, he lifted her chin and offered her a crooked smile. "I know what you need. Stay here, I'll be right back."

He teleported to the kitchen and scanned the room with no idea what he sought. Seth stood in front of the refrigerator with the door open. His brother glanced at him over his shoulder. "Hungry?"

Ty shook his head. "Not for me." He paused for a moment before adding, "Comfort food."

Seth closed the fridge door with a laugh. "You need comfort food?"

Ty growled. "I said it's wasn't for me."

Just then Gwen entered the kitchen. When she got close to them, Ty reached out without thinking and gently gripped her wrist. Her eyes grew large and he could smell the hint of panic in her scent along with something else.

Seth shifted from foot to foot beside him. "Ty, man…"

His warning was cut off when something slammed into Ty's back sending him flying into the formal dining room. He crashed into the wall with Markus holding him off the floor by the throat. "What the fuck?"

Markus's dragon looked out from his eyes. Pissed off didn't begin to describe it. Gwen ran up beside them, grabbing his forearm. "Markus, please. He meant no harm. Look at him. Really look at him."

After a long moment, his dragon eyes shifted back to human and he reached up and removed Ty's sunglasses. Ty expected Gwen to react, but she didn't. Then again, he didn't dare look at her with the mood Markus was in. "I wanted to ask Gwen what kinds of comfort foods she liked."

It sounded so lame he started laughing. An instant later, his body relaxed, almost sagging into his brother. Then laughter overtook him.

Markus released him, letting Ty fall to the floor. "What the hell is wrong with you?"

Ty shook his head. "Comfort food." He took a deep breath and stopping laughing. "What's wrong with you?"

"Gwen's pregnant." Ty, his brothers and Gwen turned toward Ash's voice at the entrance of the dining room. Frowning, Ty glanced back to Gwen, then Markus. All humor faded from him. There was one thing their dragons wouldn't tolerate—another touching their pregnant mate, which Ty knew firsthand. Sophia wasn't even his mate and he'd hated seeing Garrick with her.

Ty stood. "Fuck. Man, if I knew…"

Markus didn't reply at first. He stood between Ty and Ash like he watched a tennis match. Just when Ty was about lose his patience, Markus smiled, wide. "I'll be damned. You've started the mating dance."

About to argue with his brother, Ty locked gazes with Ash and knew Markus was right. When in Hades had he allowed it to happen?

CHAPTER FOURTEEN

They'd blinded him. No, *Elizabeth* did this to him. The liquid she dropped in his eyes burned like the fires in Tartarus. Hours later, he lay on the damned steel table, strapped down like a rabid animal, unable to see anything but shadows and the bright-ass fucking light.

The click of the door made him jerk his head. The silhouette of the female his dragon wanted to tear apart entered the room. Elizabeth, he remembered from when he lived in Olympus with his brothers, possessed a darkness that rivaled Garrick's rage.

She halted next to him, looking down on him. Damn, he wished he could see her face to get a better reading on what she had planned. No doubt she'd come to gloat on her handiwork or perhaps to torture him some more.

Yet, she never asked him for information about his

brothers or the gods. In fact, she didn't ask him anything, just taunted and caused him pain. *Twisted bitch.*

"Oh, you're awake. I feared I'd lost you."

There was a smile in her tone. He growled and jerked his arms against the chains holding him to the table. "Bitch."

"Now, now. Flattery will get you nowhere. Do you know why you're here, dear?"

"Because you're a psychotic bitch," he growled and turned his head straight at the ceiling.

Her tone remained void of emotion as she continued to talk as if he'd said nothing. "I loved you before Sophia sank her claws into you. The daemon had no right to come to Olympus and taint you and your brothers with her false friendship. Then you had to fill her with a child."

Ty snapped his gaze back to her, relieved his vision had finally started to clear. Only he and Sophia knew the child was his. "You can't know for sure."

Her laugh was bitter and loud. "I had my suspicions, but it wasn't until Sophia fought for her last breaths while I extracted the child from her womb I knew for sure. It was your name on her lips when she died."

"You bitch!" He yanked his arms up to grab her, but the chains stopped him. Fury burned in his veins, fed by the surfacing pain of the loss of his friend and the mother of his child. His dragon roared in his head and together they fought against the bindings until, one-by-one, they snapped. Ty lunged for Elizabeth and grabbed her by the neck. Her eyes grew round a split second before everything went black.

Ty woke with a start, fear and anger racing through him. The first thing he saw was Ash's concerned emerald-green eyes studying him from above. She had her hands on his arms as if holding him to the bed. "What...? What happened?"

"You were dreaming."

Taking a deep, shaky breath, he scanned his surroundings. *His bedroom.* He was in his room, his bed, with Ash. Not in the torture room with Elizabeth. When Ash released him, he instantly hugged her close and kissed the top of her head. His whole body shook as the rush of adrenaline faded.

"Elizabeth killed Sophia."

Ash raised her head to stare at him. "You're sure?"

He nodded. "It was the last thing she said to me before I lost it. I was pissed she tortured me, but when she admitted to killing Sophia and taking Amissa from her, I couldn't control the dragon's rage any longer. I killed her, Ash."

She shook her head. "Tell me about the dream."

He closed his eyes, not wanting to relive the nightmare, but he had to tell her. After all, she was sent here to judge him. The gods would probe her mind to seek the truth she learned. Hiding things from her would only hurt them both in the end. She didn't deserve to be punished because of his arrogance.

For the first time on over five hundred years, he wanted to trust a female, wanted to trust Ash. Because, like it or not, she was his mate and he was falling for her.

After he spilled the whole dream-flashback to her, he felt as if a weight was lifted from his chest. "I have to have killed her."

"Not necessarily."

"What do you mean?"

"The dream cut off before she died. Elle's painting showed Garrick standing in front of you with the divine dagger. So, until we find out for sure how Elizabeth died, I'm not giving up. Besides, we're closer to building a case to clear your name." A smile formed on her lips said she was up to something.

"How so?"

"Elizabeth admitted to killing Sophia. Zeus wants her killer punished more than Elizabeth's. Even if you did kill her, Zeus would see it as justified."

He doubted it, but it sparked a small amount of hope. "Won't we need proof?"

"Yeah, and we'll work on that. At least we have more to go on." She pushed up and crawled off the bed.

He watched as she dressed. "Where are you going?"

"To speak with Thea and Ariel. You should let Markus know." Then she turned and rushed out the door before he could protest or ask any more questions.

Blowing out a breath, he sat up and slid into a pair of jeans before heading out to find Markus and his brothers. It was time to call dear old dad and get some answers.

NIKALOS LEANED against the dirt covered stone wall of wherever the hell Garrick had moved him. The dickhead said it would be a more permanent home for Nik and the other prisoners. The place smelled like damp dirt and rock, telling him they could be inside a cave or in an underground cavern.

How many years had it been since Tyson escaped thanks to one of his brothers? Nik lost track of time long ago. Besides, he really didn't expect the Sons of War— his brothers—to come back for him. The number one reason? Garrick cast a memory spell over Ty just moments before Zavier burst through the place like a F5 tornado.

Since then, Garrick had moved Nik and the others around every few months. The bastard was paranoid to the extreme.

His paranoia was why Nik failed to tell his dear brother the serum he used to keep him from shifting into his dragon no longer worked like it once had. Nik guessed it would take a few weeks to a month before he regained enough strength to make the shift. Just as long as Garrick didn't figure out the serum was useless.

The echo of footsteps sounded off the wall, drawing a growl from him. A moment later, Garrick emerged from the dark corridor with a smirk on his face. "Are you comfortable, brother?"

"You lost the privilege to call me brother the day you turned on Ares and the rest of us."

"Ah. And where are your brothers? Oh, that's right. They rescued Tyson and left you behind." He stalked to the right side of the cave and pulled something from a basketball size hole in the stone wall.

Nik let out another growl. His brothers didn't know he was here. He knew as much when he tried to communicate with Ty during his captivity. The male didn't recognize his voice or his name. No surprise there, since Elizabeth kept him shackled and drugged the whole time. Then there was the memory spell Garrick put on him.

Tracking Garrick as he crossed the small room-like space, Nik rose to his feet and paced to the bars. Peering into the cell next to his, he saw a female gripping onto the bars. With wide eyes, she watched Garrick approach her.

Garrick smiled at her. "Are you ready now, Blair?"

At her nod, Garrick opened the cell and she stepped out, giving Nik full view of her. His dragon roared within and the man jerked on the bars while cursing his twisted, psychotic sorry-ass brother. "You sick bastard! She's a child!"

Garrick growled. "Blair, tell him how old you are."

"Seventeen."

"A child, you sick fuck."

Garrick waved him away and handed the girl an amber-colored vile. "She's a very powerful child. She's the granddaughter of Themis and so is her older sister. Once I have both of them working for me, I'll have the power to change the divine laws and become the new king of the gods."

The male was truly insane. Themis was the goddess of divine law. With two of her descendants under Garrick's wing, he could overturn the current power in Olympus. Nik let out another, louder growl. Looked like he would have to break out sooner than he thought.

When the girl, Blair, took the vial and drank it, Nik screamed at Garrick to stop and threw himself into the bars of his cage. Blair dropped the glass and doubled over. Garrick picked her up and carried her out of the room.

Fury clawed at his insides, enraging his dragon even more. They could do what they wished to him, but when it came to innocent people—especially children—Nik couldn't stand by and watch and wait.

He had to find a way out of the damned cage.

CHAPTER FIFTEEN

Garrick laid the girl on the sofa in a small cabin a few yards from the cave where he kept Nik. The cabin served as his temporary home as well as his office until his Imperials finished construction on the new command center.

Studying the girl sleeping on the couch, he scowled. None of the other descendants passed out during the process. Maybe he'd given her too much of the serum.

"Into harvesting children now?"

Garrick growled at the deep voice from behind him. "This is not your concern, Eros."

"Maybe not." The god of love and desire drifted around the room until he stopped at the bedroom door.

Garrick faced Eros full on and narrowed his gaze upon him, suspicion creeping up his spine. "What do you want?"

"Your minions failed. Again."

Fisting his hands at his sides, Garrick counted silently in his head. Losing his shit with the god was not wise. Especially if Garrick wanted his plan to be successful. He'd need Cupid on his side to make it happen.

"I'm well aware." Motioning to Blair still sleeping on the sofa, Garrick allowed his lips to lift in a small smile of achievement. "She is my ticket to ruling Olympus."

Eros flicked his gaze from the child back to Garrick and snarled. "I can't allow you to do that. It would disrupt the balance between the worlds."

Blah, blah, blah. Garrick had heard it all before. It was the same fucking speech Markus feed him for centuries. *A bunch of shit.* "The child is the granddaughter of Themis."

Eros's gaze fell on Blair once more. "She's too young. Even with her goddess half unlocked, she won't fully come into her powers until she reaches the age of twenty-five."

Suppressing the urge to throw a fireball at the god, Garrick turned toward the kitchen to grab a beer. "She will lead me to her sister, who *is* of age."

Why the hell was he bothering with explanations? Oh, yes, because he need Eros and he was the only god he could persuade to his side. Desire was a strong power after all. "You could join me and take your rightful place as next on the throne."

"Why should I help you?"

Pulling a beer from the fridge, Garrick grinned. "You would have the power to bring down the Sons of War and avenge Elizabeth's death lawfully, without a trial."

Eros let out a bitter, humorless laugh. "I'm bringing Tyson down for her death."

The idea did intrigue the god. Garrick could sense it in the way the male's scent changed at the mention of having the power to take down Ty. So he threw him another little piece of information to chew on. "I have in my possession the divine dagger and two very powerful weavers fully capable of harvesting the gods' powers and containing them until we find the right candidates to hold the power."

Eros froze and stared at him for a long moment as if considering his options. "How do I know you speak the truth?"

Garrick reached behind him, pulled out the dagger from its sheath at his back, and held it out between them. "The weavers are isolated and cloaked from the gods and my brothers. They have already prepared the spell and the containment unit."

Amusement along with greed lit the blue depths of Eros's gaze as he stepped forward. When he reached out for the dagger, Garrick snatched it back and slipped it back inside the sheath.

Locking gazes with Garrick, Eros smiled coolly. "You have it all figured out, don't you?"

"I like being prepared. With or without you, I will not fail."

T<small>Y</small> <small>ENTERED</small> the great room and met Gwen's gaze. He broke the eye contact to search his surroundings. Aphrodite sat at the piano with a smile on her face and Elle sat next to Gwen on the sofa. Yet, there was no sign of his brothers. "Where's Markus? And the weaver? You found one, right?"

Gwen gestured to the chair across from her. "Please sit and relax. Markus should be here anytime. Yes, we found a weaver."

He strode over to the chair and sat. The feeling of shock coming from Aphrodite made his lips lift in a slight smile. "Have you given up on me so fast, goddess?"

"Of course not. I'm amazed at how calm you are in a room full of women."

Letting out a low, playful growl, he drummed his fingers on the arms of the chair, not knowing how much of the silence he could take. The goddess of love was wrong. Calm was far from what he felt. In fact, he was about to jump up and go for a run or something. The mansion was too quiet, yet there were people every-where. His daughter and Cyrus rested in their rooms. He could feel Ash somewhere with the nymphs. Maxwell was in the kitchen, most likely preparing for lunch. All the quiet made him edgy. Well, edgier than normal.

He should be used to the quiet. He'd craved it at one time. Since Ash entered his life and he realized she was his mate, his outlook on the world changed. He had a new purpose, a renewed hope he might just make it out of the whole damned mess alive. He actually cared. It was Ash's doing. Her inability to give up on him pushed him find the answers he'd avoided for far too long.

The sound of the front door opening and closing followed by two sets of footsteps made him jump to his feet. When he turned to the foyer, he froze. The petite redhead dressed in faded blue jeans and a green top stared at him while she held a toddler in her arms. The female resembled Sophia in so many ways, she could be a daughter or sister. She also favored Amissa in looks, only shorter.

Markus stepped forward, blocking the female from Ty's view. Meeting his brother's glare, Ty asked, "Who is she?"

Markus growled. "Be aware of yourself, brother."

Ty rolled his eyes. "Do you realize who she looks like?"

Markus paused, then glanced at the female over his shoulder. "Sophia came to mind when I first saw her, but she is not her."

"How can you be sure?" Ty lowered his voice to a level only Markus could hear with the impeccable hearing they possessed as dragon-shifters.

"I'm not. It doesn't matter right now. She is here and is under our protection. She is also the weaver we seek," Markus countered, then walked passed him.

Ty studied the weaver for a moment before speaking. "I'm Ty."

She gave a nod and rubbed small circles on the child's back. "I'm Selene."

"Ty?"

He turned toward Gwen. Her lips lifted in a soft smile. Warmth grew inside his chest and spread. The minor goddess of love had found a way inside his heart. It was odd how he felt connected to her, much like the blood bond he shared with his brothers. Maybe because she and Markus were bonded mates…?

Stepping to the side, he motioned to Selene toward the great room. Disbelief still churned within him. How could she look so much like Sophia and not be her?

As he followed behind her, her son stared at him with interest. Ty smiled at him. In return the child smiled back right before he buried his face in his mother's shoulder. A sense of nervousness surrounded the child. The slight fear on his scent and way he clung to Selene, especially when he or Markus were close, told Ty the boy had witnessed things no child should see.

No doubt Garrick had something to do with it. After all Selene favored Sophia in looks and was a powerful weaver—another thing Ty clued into the moment he saw her. He hadn't seen a magical signature so bright and strong from anyone before. Then again, he'd not encountered many weavers.

Instead of taking a seat, he stood with his back against the wall next to the bar tucked in the far corner of the great room. Beside him were the French doors that lead out onto the patio overlooking the backyard. Seth, Zavier, and Drake entered and took their usual spots at the bar. His brothers remained quiet as they studied Selene, sending him curious glances, which he ignored. Even Seth seemed to be a loss for words, making Ty wonder if there was something wrong with him.

Aphrodite glided over to Selene, arms extended to the boy in her arms. "May I?"

Selene nodded and allowed the goddess to take her son. Aphrodite smiled wide. "What's his name?"

"Trenton."

"What a beautiful, yet strong, name for a handsome little man." Aphrodite motioned toward the empty seat on the sofa next to Gwen. "Please have a seat."

The goddess took Trenton over to the piano where she sat him on her lap and began to play a soft classical tune Ty didn't recognize.

"Ares." Markus's deep boomed through the room, drawing everyone's attention.

A moment later, the god of war appeared in the middle of the room, his gaze instantly falling on Selene. "I see you found a weaver."

On the heels of his statement, Ares focused on

Gwen. His lips twitched slightly before he turned his attention to Markus. "Eros's patience grows thin."

Ty snorted. "Yes, I've already had a little visit from Cupid. Then Amissa was attacked in her home by Imperials."

Markus spoke up next. "That seems too much of a coincidence. Do you know if he and Garrick have teamed up?"

Ares folded his arms over his chest and glanced to Aphrodite, who pretended not to pay attention to them. Ty guessed he didn't blame her. Eros was her son. "I'm not his keeper. But I have noticed he hasn't been around much. It's perfectly reasonable he'd go to Garrick to get at you. Where is Amissa?"

Ty set his jaw and considered not answering his father's question. The problem was Ares knew she was inside the mansion. "She is resting. Did you know Garrick has the divine dagger?"

Narrowing his eyes, Ares studied Ty for several moments. "Not possible."

Elle stood up and paced to the covered painting in the corner to Ares's left Ty hadn't noticed before. With a quick jerk, she uncovered it and stepped back. Ares unfolded his arms and advanced toward the painting. As if transfixed, he didn't speak for a few moments. When he turned back to them, Ty saw the fury burning in his black eyes.

"Tyson, is the scene accurate?"

"I believe so, but I'm not a hundred percent. That's

the reason we sought out a weaver. Ash has a theory Garrick killed Elizabeth and placed a memory spell over me to make me believe I did it." Ty fisted his hands. Ares, as a god and his father, knew what he'd gone through.

"I don't know as much as you think. I only know what I can pull from your thoughts. The power to see into the future is not one of my gifts. Those are reserved for the Fates and their children." Ares gave a pointed stare at Elle, and then Gwen.

Seth cursed from his bar stool. "Of fucking course. Elle is the daughter of Nyx. The Fates are daughters of Nyx."

"It doesn't necessarily mean that is why she has visions, right?" Gwen asked.

Ares shrugged. "In her case, yes, she did get the visions from Nyx. However, it is possible Nyx gifted her with the sight and it could be limited. We won't really know until she comes into her powers."

Next to Ty at the bar, Zavier shifted on his stool, but said nothing. All the signs were there, Ty noted. His brother's inability to stay away from Elle, yet the frustration flowing around him said the male battled some kind of internal conflict. A conflict Ty knew too well— Zavier was fighting the urge to mate.

Ty would leave it alone because his brother had to solve his own issues. Besides, Ty had his hands full with Ash.

"What about the dagger?" Markus asked, bringing the meeting back to the main issue.

Ares shook his head. "It's not possible for Garrick to have it. I just came from meeting with Hades and he assured me the dagger is being protected by the *drakon* Zander."

Zander was the son of Typhon, brother of Sophia, and a two-headed serpent-like dragon who lived in the Underworld and protected the divine dagger. *Drakons* were born dragons able to take human form whereas the Sons of War were earth-born immortal men who possessed the dragon spirit of the Drakon Ismenios, making them dragon-shifters.

Although Zander was a wanderer and not very sane. Ty growled. "Does Hades know where Zander is?"

Ares growled back. "He couldn't confirm his location."

Fuck. Shit just kept getting deeper…

Markus cleared his throat. "My head is starting to ache. Let's deal with one issue at a time. Selene is here to help unlock Ty's memories and in exchange she is under our protection from the Imperials. They killed her husband about six months ago. I'm guessing they are looking for her and her son."

Ty nodded. "When and where do we do this? I'm tired of losing my shit every time I have a flashback. Speaking of which, Elizabeth admitted to me she killed Sophia."

Aphrodite jumped up from the bench at the piano,

holding a sleeping Trenton in her arms, and faced him. "Are you sure?"

"Yes."

"This changes things. It doesn't matter if you killed Elizabeth. Zeus will consider it a public service. Your duties were to track down her killer and keep a new war from starting." Aphrodite frowned at her words. Sadness and a sense of relief drifted from her thick and frequent. "I'm sorry my granddaughter caused you so much pain."

Ty held the goddess's gaze for several moments before he pushed off the wall and paced over to her. Dipping his head, he kissed on the cheek. "Elizabeth was lost to her power of desire. She was no longer the granddaughter you knew and loved."

With tears in her eyes, Aphrodite cupped his right cheek, purposely touching the scar peeking from under his shades. "I know. That's what saddens me so. She was filled with jealousy and allowed her desire for power to rule her. I am happy you are whole again."

He laughed softly. "I'll never be whole again, but I'm learning to love again."

She glanced over his shoulder a second before Ash pressed into him from behind and wrapped her arms around his waist. "We just need a witness to Elizabeth's admission."

"What about Nik? Have you figured out where he is?"

Ty turned to Markus and shook his head. "No."

Ares stilled, his body going taught and fisted his hands. "Nikolas?"

The bastard must have pulled out the memory from Ty's thoughts just then. "Stay out of my head. Where is Nikolas?"

"Fuck if I know. I lost contact with him about four years ago. I never thought too much about it. After all he was known for hiding out and making me track him down. Only this time I didn't bother. Too much going on with Garrick to invest energy to Nik's games."

Renewed hope bloomed in Ty's chest. Nik was in the room the whole time Ty was there. He knew this because he felt the male's presence when he was awake. "Can you track him now?"

"Sure. It may take a few hours, but I can track any of my sons."

Ty ground his molars together to keep from starting a verbal war with his father. The bastard could have found him and had his brothers get him a lot sooner. Then again, if that happened, would he have found out Elizabeth was Sophia's murderer?

Seth stood and stretched. "What about your memories?"

Ty glanced at Selene and shrugged. "I'd like to get them back of course, but it'll have to wait until after we find Nik and bring him home."

Ash squeezed him a little harder and kissed his shoulder blade. He circled an arm around her and twisted to face her. "Thank you."

She smiled and pressed her lips to his. "Just doing my job."

He bit down on her lower lip, making her moan softly. "I'll repay you for that later. Now we have work to do."

CHAPTER SIXTEEN

Ty materialized outside a cave in the Rocky Mountains. The smell of damp rock and earth differed from his time of captivity. Which meant Garrick moved the location. No surprise there. It was actually one of the smartest things he'd done. Although he hadn't taken into consideration Ares might help them locate their brother.

Markus and Seth took form next to him. Together they entered the cave and instantly Ty felt a familiar presence, a draw to someone he should know. He took off down the corridor to his left. All the while his brothers' footfalls against the stone floor sounded behind him, closing in.

About twenty feet inside the cave hallway, an opening came into view. A soft, dim light spilled out into the hallway. The scents coming from the room was like a slap in the face, bringing back the rage and the memories of being helpless chained to the steel table. Ty let out a growl that echoed off the stone walls.

Rushing into the circular room, Ty could barely contain his anger. Cages lined the far wall, two of them occupied. One was a male he assumed was Nik. "Nikalos?"

The male raised his head and met Ty's gaze. His lips curled into a grin while his brows lifted in a challenge. "It is nice of my brothers to finally come for me."

"I don't have time for arrogance." Ty said as he ripped the lock from the cage and opened the barred door. "Let's get the hell out of here. You can state your complaints later."

Nik stood from where he sat on the floor and stalked to the door. But instead of leaving with them he moved to a cage a few feet from his where a small form laid curled up in the corner was. When Nik broke the lock, darted inside and came back with a teenage girl in his arms, Ty's anger flood him like hot liquid filling his veins. "She's a child," he growled.

Nik nodded and continued out of the cave, forcing Ty and the others to follow. "Yeah. Our brother is a sick fuck."

"What's wrong with her?"

"Garrick injected her with some kind of serum. She's been asleep for more than ten hours."

Bastard. At one time Ty had hoped his brother could be brought back from his insanity and make amends for his crimes, but not now. Garrick stooped to a new low with kidnapping children and trying to unlock their powers before they were ready.

About ten feet from the exit, about a dozen Imperials stormed into the cavern, blocking them. Ty skidded to a halt. Markus and Seth step up beside him, shielding Nik and the girl. *Mark, can you teleport?*

Markus growled, rumbling the building and the floor. *No. The bastard's got a spell on the place.*

Lifting his hands waist high, Ty curled his fingers, formed a baseball-size fireball and thrust it at the Imperials. As expected, the cowards jumped back from the exit.

Ty charged ahead and, once outside, threw another fireball at the group to their right, making them scramble out of the way. Nik took the chance to dart off toward the woods with the child. Seth followed, leaving Markus and Ty to deal with the idiot-with-power gain. Which was fine by Ty. It'd been a while since he'd had a really good workout.

A couple of the Imperials darted to the side to chase Nik, but Markus was faster. He grabbed them by the backs of neck and slammed their heads together. The crack of their skulls echoed off the trees and rocks around them.

With efficient, swift grace, Ty advanced on the group of demi-gods who stood in defensive stances. He plowed into a group of four, knocking them down like they were cardboard cutouts. *What the fuck?*

He scanned the faces of the others, who all stared off

into the darkening forest. *Empty shells. Puppets.* Only able to only obey their string holder. An icy sensation rolled down his spine a split second before a female scream cut through the air.

Markus heard it too and took off in the direction Nik and Seth had gone. Ty followed, running in time with his brother, heart pounding and the burn of fear for the girl racing in his blood. *May the gods help anyone who lays a hand on her.*

They came to a stop next to Seth and Nik. In front of them, Garrick held the girl in his grasp, fear widening her eyes.

Garrick grinned. "What a happy family reunion."

Markus let out a deep, fierce growl. "Let the girl go. She's of no use to you."

"That is where you are wrong. Blair, here, will lead me to her big sister."

Dread sliced through Ty's gut. Garrick had to be talking about Rayna, one of the women on the list Gwen found among her father's notes. Garrick could never be allowed to capture the female. Next to him, Seth growled loud and long and charged forward. Before he reached Garrick, the bastard disappeared, taking Blair with him.

Seth let out a roar. The ground shook and birds fled the treetops. Markus slammed a hand on Seth's shoulder. "We'll find them."

Nik raked a hand through his hair. "Blair is very weak at the moment. Garrick will need to allow her to build up her strength. I'm guessing because her age, the serum he gave her to unlock her powers doesn't work the way it does on older descendants."

Ty nodded. He didn't like leaving her in the hands of Garrick, but Nik was right. It'd be at least a week before Garrick would send Blair after her sister. Right now, they needed to prepare for his judgment day.

ASH CLOSED the door to Amissa's room just as she sensed Ty entering the mansion with his brothers. There was another presence with them. *Nikalos*. She descended the stairs and followed the loud voices coming from the great room.

Ty met her gaze instantly and he stalked toward her. Drawing her into a tight hug, he buried his nose into her neck. She hugged him back, feeling the slight tremor going through him he hid from everyone around him.

"What happened?" she whispered.

He lifted his head and held her gaze through his shades. "Garrick has one of Themis's daughters. She's only seventeen."

Fury rose within Ash and nudged her to find Garrick and rip his head off. *Be done with the damn thing.* "He'll use her to get to Rayna."

Ty pulled his back slightly to study her for a moment. "You know who Themis's daughters are?"

Ash rolled her eyes and pushed away from him. "I

was raised in Olympus and researched the archives to learn everything I could about descendants as well as the Sons. Yes, I know. I will also remind you I spent two years with Garrick, learning everything I could about the women he had on his top ten list."

She walked past him and stopped in front of Nik. "Were you there when Elizabeth admitted to killing Sophia?"

Nik nodded and crossed his arms. "I was. The bitch got what she deserved. But I was surprised Garrick showed up with the dagger and literally stabbed her in the back."

Ash froze. Okay, she hadn't expected so much anger from the dragon. Then again, he'd been a prisoner in the same room Ty was tortured in. A wave of relief washed over her knowing that Nik was on their side. Glancing over her shoulder, she smiled at Ty who stared at Nik, disbelief etched in his handsome features.

"Markus, can you have Selene prepare to unlock Ty's memories? Once it is done, I have to take him to Olympus for judgment." With hope it was almost over, she paced to Ty and kissed him.

Breaking the kiss, she removed his shades. "We have a witness and, with your memories unlocked, Zeus has to drop the charges on you."

Ty dropped his gaze back to her lips. "I'm not counting on it until I hear him say the words."

"Fair enough. For now, I'm hungry. Care to dine with me?"

The brow over his good eye—the human eye—rose and his lips curved into a sensual, yet naughty smile. "I'll have Maxwell bring dinner to our room."

Her heart skipped a beat. "*Our* room?"

"Yep, I've been an ass and denied what is fated for too long. You're mine and I want to seal the deal."

CHAPTER SEVENTEEN

The open-mouth look of surprise on Ash's face sent a smug and satisfying thrill straight to his heart. He'd known for a while how she felt about him—how she never gave up on him and fought his daemons when he wanted to throw in the towel. Her belief gave him strength when he needed something to cling to. For years, he lived with the knowledge judgment would come. Now, he actually believed he could walk away a free man.

He owed his thanks to Ash—his mate and his heart.

He teleported to his room—no, *their* room. When they materialized in the middle of the large bedroom, he did something he swore he'd never do. He confessed his love for the female in his arms. "I love you, Ashlynn, goddess of the hunt, and want you as my bonded mate for all eternity." Tears filled her eyes, making his heart ache. "Don't cry. You're not allowed to cry."

She laughed as a single tear rolled down her cheek and cupped his face in her hands. "Only happy tears with you. I've loved you from the moment I saw you, but didn't realize it until the first time we spoke outside this room. I am yours, always, and accept the mating."

He struck fast and hard, sinking his teeth into her shoulder. She sucked in a hiss, then moaned and melted into him. Her blood coated his tongue, tangy and sweet like wine. Her scent surrounded him, invading his head with its drugging, strawberry fragrance.

Tightening his grip, Ty tugged her closer and still she wasn't close enough. He withdrew his fangs from her and walked her backward. When her legs hit the mattress, she fell on it. A moment later both their clothes dematerialized and Ash smiled, showing the tips of small, sharp fangs. As a goddess, Ty didn't have to cut himself for her to complete the blood exchange. No, she could give herself fangs to score his skin. His cock jerked at the thought of her taking from him. Her lashes lowered, then lifted as she gazed up at him. In the next instant, she gripped his cock at the base and covered him with her mouth.

Pleasure slammed into him, damn near making him come. Her warm, wet mouth moved over his dick, sucking and licking. He sank his fingers into her silky red hair and tugged, but she dug her nails into the backs of his thighs, intensifying the building wave of pleasure. Then she sank her tiny fangs into his cock.

Fuck.

The sting of the bite quickly turned to pleasure as she continued to work him with her mouth. The orgasm slammed into him, making him lose all conscious thought. When the last shudder rocked through him, he withdrew and gazed down at Ash, his lids heavy.

"Get on your hands and knees in the middle of the bed."

The sweet scent of her desire reached out to him, driving him and the dragon insane. She scrambled farther up on the bed and positioned herself. He crawled up behind her, leaned down and nipped her ass cheek. She whimpered lifted her hips.

Slowly, he trailed kisses up her back until his body hovered over hers. He traced a hand up her outer thigh to her hip around to belly, and then lower. A small cry of pleasure burst from her lips when he cupped her pussy. He slipped two fingers into her wet folds and stroked, increasing the rhythm until the juices from her orgasm coated his fingers.

Withdrawing his finger, he sank his cock inside her in one swift thrust. Damn, this female belonged to him, was inside him. With each passing minute, his connection to her spread inside him and their bond grew stronger. It was as if the missing piece of his soul had been found.

Biting down her ear lobe, he spoke in a husky, growly tone. "You are mine."

"Yes." Her breathless response sent a jolt straight to

his cock, pushing him closer to the edge with each thrust.

She reached up and tangled her fingers in his hair. Fisting a handful, she moved her hips in time with his. Pleasure rolled through the strengthening mating bond. Ash screamed out her release. He followed her over the edge.

Ty fell to the bed on his side, taking Ash with him. Just as he got comfortably curled around her, a knock sounded on the door. Ash wiggled as if she was going to get up, but Ty locked his arms around her. "Whoever it is, they'll leave."

"It may be our dinner."

Ty growled and sniffed the air. Maxwell's scent lingered from the other side of the door. Reluctantly, he rose from the bed and answered the door, not bothering to put his clothes on.

Two hours later, Ash sat on the sofa in the study watching Selene direct a blindfolded Ty to a chair in the middle of the room. Next to her, Gwen covered her hand. Ash smiled and opened then closed her hand over the other woman's.

"Ashlynn." Ty growled out in warning as Selene helped him sit in the chair.

A laugh bubbled up at Ty's warning. He hadn't called her by her birth name in about a week, she realized. Biting her lower lip, she tried not to laugh. She really didn't know what got into her.

Gwen leaned into her and whispered, "You're nervous. It's natural."

Nodding, Ash took a deep breath, calming her nerves. She was so not helping the situation. Any anxiety she felt traveled through the mating bond, in turn putting Ty on edge.

"What's the point of the blindfold?" Ash whispered back to her friend.

Selene answered instead. "It lets me know how much he can trust me. In order for this to work, he has to completely open his mind to me."

The weaver glanced toward the door and allowed her gaze to linger for a long moment before focusing back on Ty. Ash thought she was having second thoughts until Thea entered with Trenton in her arms, the toddler fast asleep with his head on her shoulder.

Selene smiled and her body sagged as if relieved to see her son. Nodding to the nymph as she sat in a chair in the corner of the study, Selene removed Ty's blindfold. He blinked several times before locking gazes with Ash. The pupil of his right eye—the dragon's eye—shrank to a thin line, leaving the red and gold iris.

"Ty, I need you to focus on this pendent." Selene held up a silver chain with a large teardrop-shaped crystal at the end. As she moved the pendent side to side, she spoke in a hushed, clear tone. "This is similar to hypnosis, but I won't take you all the way under. I need you awake when I cast the spell. Do you understand?"

When he nodded and watched the crystal, she continued. "Listen to only my voice and relax." Another short pause while all sound in the room dissipated, leaving the hum of Markus's computer running. "What is the last thing you remember before seeing Elizabeth at the bar?"

Ash's heart thumped rapidly in her throat. She and Ty had talked about this and agreed she needed to be in the room since she was the jury, so to speak. Jealousy would not rear its ugly head, Ash wouldn't allow it. Besides, she needed to know everything that happened between him and Elizabeth before, during, and after the whole ordeal.

Yet, when Ty started to speak, Ash squeezed Gwen's hand a little tighter. Her new friend just patted their linked hands with her free one.

"Zavier, Seth and I went to the pub in town to wind down after a fight with Imperials. I saw her walk into the bar. Although her magical signature told me she was a minor goddess, I didn't know who she was. However, I was drawn to her..." He paused with his brows drawn together. His forehead crinkled as if he was fighting some kind of internal battle with his mind.

Selene placed a hand on his shoulder. He jerked in his seat, but the weaver kept her hand where it rested. "Was she your mate?"

There was a long moment before he answered. "I believed so, at the time."

Behind his desk, Markus let out a low curse. Instantly Selene raised her hand in the air to silence him. "Go on, Ty. What happened next?"

"I bought her a drink and we played pool, laughed, and I left with her." He stopped and flung his hands to his head, pain etched in his features.

Ash's vision blurred as his pain reached her through their bond. She wanted to stop this, stop the pain he experienced. Yet, she couldn't do it. The only thing she could do was to send him a mental caress through the mating bond, letting him know she was still here.

He seemed to relax a little. Then Selene placed a hand on his forehead and began to chant something too soft for Ash to make out the words. A moment later Ty let out a roar and doubled over, holding his head in his hands as he crumbled to the floor.

Jetting to her feet, Ash rubbed her own temples and screamed at Selene. "Stop this."

Seth grabbed her from behind and caged her inside his arms, holding her back. "We must let it take its course."

"He's hurting," she breathed.

"I know."

What seemed like minutes later, Ty stilled and the pain Ash felt earlier eased until it disappeared completely. He rolled to his back on the floor and stared up and the ceiling. "Garrick killed her with the divine dagger. I was unable to shift, but my dragon was in control of me. If he hadn't stabbed her in the heart, I would have broken her neck."

His eyes closed and he released a heavy sigh. "Her admission to killing Sophia and taking Amissa filled me with a rage like I've never felt before."

Seth released her and she flew to Ty's side, cupping his face in her hands. "Justice served. Typhon nearly tore down the walls of Tartarus with his heartache for his daughter. Zeus wants her killer known and dealt with more than Elizabeth's."

"She's right."

Ash turned as a familiar voice filled the room. Artemis and Aphrodite entered the study. "Mama, why are you here?"

Artemis held out a hand to her and she went to her mother. "It's time to bring Ty in."

Dread slammed into her. Something had happened. "Why so soon? I thought he could rest first."

Sadness reached out to Ash, making tears form. "Eros has ordered it. He claims Ty's mind is too broken and he is a threat to all of us."

Aphrodite let out a soft sob before gliding over to Ty. "Your father has confirmed my son had been in contact with Garrick."

Ty stood, conjured a pair of shades and slid them into place. Then he did something no one expected. He lowered to on knee in front of the goddess of love and took her hands in his. Resting his forehead to their hands, he asked, "What is your wish of us?"

Aphrodite sniffed and lifted her chin. "Do as you were meant to do. Protect the balance of the worlds by stopping the war at any cost. And stand up."

Once he obeyed the goddess, she dematerialized. Ty turned to Ash and held out a hand. Warmth bloomed in her chest and spread throughout her body as she stepped into his embrace. It was going to okay. It had to be.

With a short nod to Artemis, Ty said, "I'm ready."

CHAPTER EIGHTEEN

Olympus hadn't changed in the five hundred plus years since Ty had last been there. Gardens bloomed year round and the lush green landscape was perfect as it'd always been. The buildings still stood like monuments to the gods who occupied them, each one built out of white marble. Greek symbols and letters marked the temple where the gods gathered for events, gatherings, and, in his case, judgment of crimes.

The sound of his boots against the white marble tiled floor echoed as he paced down the great hall toward Zeus's throne room. His heart pounded in his ears, his chest, and his feet. For the first time in his life, he felt fear. It wasn't for his life, but his mate's.

If Zeus decided for Eros, Ash would feel his death as if it were her own. Why had he bound them together?

"Stop it," Ash growled as she squeezed his hand.

Only a small amount of fear scurried away. She

insisted on being by his side for the whole trial. As did his brothers, including Nikalos.

At the end of the hall, Ares stood at the doors, waiting, his features as blank as stone. Ty gave a nod to his father and the god opened the door. Once inside the god king's chamber, Ash released her hold on Ty's hand and took a seat between to her mother and uncle, Apollo, along the right side of the room. Ty's gaze locked with Eros, who stood to Zeus's left.

The god of love and desire narrowed his eyes as Ty's brothers took up posts behind him. "Why are they here?"

Zeus held up a hand. "Silence. Tyson, approach."

Ty advance to the stand in front of the god and knelt, bowing his head. Zeus spoke loud, his voice carrying through the room. "I've spoken to Ashlynn, daughter of Artemis. She tells me Tyson is not responsible for the death of Elizabeth, goddess of desire. Nor did he kill Sophia, daughter of Typhon. Elizabeth had confessed to the crime before her death."

Eros exploded into a string of curses. "Lies."

"Silence! You will not be warned again, Eros." After a short moment, Zeus continued. "Tyson, do you have a witness to this confession?"

"I do, my lord. It is my brother Nikalos."

Nik stepped forward. "I was being held by Garrick and in the same room during Ty's captivity and torture by Elizabeth. I heard her confession. She was jealous of Ty fathering Sophia's child."

Gasps sounded around the room. Zeus raised his hand again, calling for silence. "Tyson stand up. The case of Sophia's death has always taken precedence over all others. Her father entrusted me to keep her safe while she lived here. That trust is something I will never regain from him."

The bitter rage in his tone sent a chill down Ty's back. He'd never understood why Sophia lived in Olympus. She was a daemon after all. Once she'd told him she was on a special assignment for Zeus, but never said why or what she did for the god king.

Zeus rose from his throne and descended the stairs to stand in front of Nik. The god held out his hand, palm up. When Nik placed his hand on top of Zeus's, the god clamped his fingers around Nik's wrist. Nik jerked against the hold, then relaxed. After a moment, Zeus let go and moved to Ty and repeated the process.

The act of mind probing was as violating as it sounded. Ty hated every moment of it. Even though it wasn't painful, it was uncomfortable, like a dull pressure that was more annoyance than anything. Having Zeus inside his mind, even for a brief time, made Ty want to cleanse the inside of his head. Yet, he'd endure the memory sweep to prove he didn't have any to hide.

A long silence stretched on as Zeus slowly paced a circle around them. Dread wormed its way to the forefront of his mind. What did the god find in Nik's memories? Was it enough to clear Ty of all charges?

Ty stole a glance to Ash and wished he hadn't. She

stood rod straight. Although her features reveled nothing, her eyes told him another story. There was worry and fear in her green gaze. His heart ached. All he wanted to do was go to her and hold her.

Zeus stopped in his line of sight, narrowed his eyes then followed Ty's gaze to Ash. Eros noticed, looked from Ty to Ash, and then gave Ty a smirk. "They are bonded together as mates. Her judgment doesn't count."

No. Fuck no. Ash's mouth opened then closed as she shook her head. Ty's heart hammered in his chest.

Zeus sighed as if tired. "Ashlynn, step forward."

As she made her way to Zeus, Ty fought his dragon's need to protect his mate. The beast didn't know the meaning of logic and politeness. He'd rip the building apart to get his mate to safety, weather she needed protecting or not.

When Zeus reached for her, Ty was there, standing between them, his lips curled. Ash gripped his arm and tugged. "It's okay. I have nothing to hide. Not anymore."

She stepped around him, cupped his face, and kissed him on the lips. "Trust me," she whispered before turning to face Zeus, then held out her hand.

Ty fought for control over his impulse to break the connection between his mate and the god king. He didn't give a damn if they had to live the rest of their lives on the run.

Okay, so maybe he needed to calm the fuck down.

Zeus let go of Ash's hand, kissed her on the forehead, and stepped away. On his way to his throne, he said, "All charges against Tyson are dropped. He was not responsible for Elizabeth's death or her choice to align with Garrick and the Imperials. He did, however, help solve Sophia's death, which will get Typhon off my ass."

Eros charged at Ty, knocking him to the floor hard enough both of them slide across the marble and into a column. Knocking the god off of him, Ty jumped to his feet and crouched in a defensive stance, a fireball balanced in his palm. "It's over, Eros. You lost."

Standing, Eros glared at Ty, pain and a fierce need to revenge in his gaze. "Never. You will pay for my daughter's life."

"Eros!" Zeus's single word command boomed through the room. "Leave it. Amissa is off limits. She is Typhon's granddaughter and will be protected as such."

Eros didn't move. His chest rose and fell as he focused on Ty. "This is not over."

Then he dematerialized.

Extinguishing the fireball, Ty straightened and raked a hand through his hair. It was bad enough they had to watch for Garrick, now they also needed to keep an eye over their shoulders for Eros.

He caught Ash by the waist when she rushed to him and pulled her into a tight hug. Breathing in her scent, he calmed. "Can we go home now?"

She laughed. "Yes. Thanks the gods."

CHAPTER NINETEEN

Ash stepped out of the shower and smiled at the gorgeous male filling the doorway, waiting for her. She'd known the moment he entered the bathroom. It was when she decided to take her time. A small amount of disappointment made her frown. She'd hoped he would join her, but he didn't. "Enjoy the show?"

One corner of his sensual lips lifted. "Get dressed and meet me in the garden. I have a surprise for you."

He pushed off the doorjamb, kissed her, and left.

Odd. What could he possibly have for her in the garden?

She quickly dressed and threw her damp hair up in a ponytail. Curiosity had a grip on her now. Her dragon closed off some of his emotions to her, leaving only the love and sexual desire he felt while watching her shower through the clear curtain. Both of which kept her from being angry at his cool demeanor when she stepped out of the tub.

Cutting across the great room, she exited the French doors and turned left toward the gardens. She scented the air, drawing in the vast assortment of fragrances on the ocean breeze. A keener sense of smell was one of the benefits to bonding to Ty. With her own ability to connect to animals, she developed the ability to use the dragon's senses such as night vision and smell.

It made sense to her. After all, she was bonded to the dragon as much as the man.

A new, yet familiar scent greeted her as she approached the mini courtyard in the center of the garden. When she rounded the corner, she froze midstep.

Her father stood with his back to her, his hands tucked in the pockets of his slacks. As if sensing her, he turned. Their gazes met and hers blurred. Confusion moved in like storm clouds, the pain of his rejection still fresh on her heart.

"Why are you here?" She folded her arms across her chest and stayed where she was.

Frown lines formed on his forehead and he dropped his shoulders. "A certain dragon pointed out I'm a bitter old man and a bastard for turning away from you."

She flicked her gaze to Ty, then back to Evan. "You still didn't answer my question."

Maybe she was being childish, but she'd allowed

hope into her soul this man would welcome her with open arms. Where did it get her? Tears and the need to go home to her mother for consoling—a weakness she would not allow again.

Evan shifted from foot to foot. Sorrow and guilt drifted off him in waves, almost chokingly. He studied her for several moments before speaking. "You're right to be angry with me. I acted like an ass."

"What changed your mind?"

"Your dragon can be pretty persuasive." He pulled a hand from his pocket and held it out to her. "I was so clouded with hurt and anger, I didn't want to see what was right in front me."

She didn't move, unsure if she could trust what she was hearing. "*Mitera* believed you were dead. It pained her so much she never spoke of you."

His eyes watered. Instantly, he cleared his throat and averted his gaze. "I lived a long time cursed to this realm, believing Artemis sent me here. I guess there are a lot of unknowns. I can't take back my words, but I'd like to start over…if you'll let me."

Her nose tingled and she wiped her eyes before she rushed to him, hugging him tight. "What do we do now?"

"I need to talk to Artemis and figure out why I was cursed."

Pulling back to meet his gaze, she asked, "You don't know?"

"Not really. I was charged with treason and banned from Olympus and Artemis's life, no explanation. Zeus passed his sentence and that was it. When Artemis never came to me...I guess my imagination ran wild and I allowed anger to consume me." He released a heavy sigh and turned away from her.

"I told her you are still alive."

He whirled back around, his mouth working, but no words came out. Running a hand through his hair, he let out a soft curse. "I bet the way I reacted to first seeing you doesn't make her want to come running."

"She'll need time. I'll talk with her."

"Thank you." He paused and looked at his watch. "I should be getting back. Can I call you?"

Smiling, she stepped forward and hugged him. "Of course. We have much to catch up on."

When she stepped out of his embrace, he cupped her cheek. "You are as beautiful as your *mitera*."

Then he dematerialized.

Ty came up behind her and enveloped her in his arms. "He has his powers, just not his god status, nor can he enter Olympus."

Ash nodded still staring at the spot her father stood moments ago. Snapping out of the dazed state, she turned in Ty's arms and wrapped hers around his neck. She studied him through the shades then kissed him. His arms tightened around her, drawing their bodies together. When he slid his tongue inside her mouth, she moaned and fisted a handful of his hair. A growl rumbled from his throat right before the world around them shifted.

She opened her eyes and noticed they were no longer in the gardens, but their bedroom. Lifting the hem of his shirt, she jerked it over his head, discarding the cotton fabric with a toss over her shoulder. Then she pressed her lips to his chest, nipping her way down as she dropped to her knees.

"I love you," she said with her fingers working the button and zipper of his jeans.

His response was more of a half-growl, half-moan as she gripped his cock. "Love you always."

When she took him into her mouth, he hissed out a breath and tangled his fingers in her hair. She rolled his balls into her hand as she sucked. He pumped his hips in rhythm with her until he jerked back and lifted her off the ground.

She willed her clothes off with her mind and wrapped her legs around him, making him thrust inside her. Pleasure mounted within as he lifted and lowered her over his cock, each thrust harder and faster than the last. Sinking her nails into his shoulder, she cried out in bliss as she came.

Ty followed shortly afterward with his own release.

He moved them to bed and tucked her against him. She sighed and snuggled into his warmth and his spicy, sage scent. "You are mine."

Laughing, he gently slapped her ass. "And you are mine as well."

Smiling, she closed her eyes and wanted to freeze time, to forever be in the arms of her mate. She had her dragon and would never let go of him.

The End

ARTEMIS'S HUNT

A DRAGONS OF ARES NOVELLA

ARTEMIS'S HUNT

A Dragons of Ares novella
Also book one in the spin off series, Gods and Dragons

UNTITLED

Artemis's Hunt

Artemis, goddess of the hunt, has lived with heartache for the last fifteen hundred years, believing her only love is dead. That's what her father—Zeus, king of the gods—told her. After recent events brought the truth to light, Artemis must gather the courage to face her lost love again.

Evangelos, former god of messengers, was content living in the mortal world until he discovered he has a daughter and her mother is Artemis. When the goddess shows up at his place of employment with tales of renewing his god status, he's skeptical. Zeus wouldn't reverse the curse out of the goodness of his heart. There is always a catch. The god king wants something in return.

When Artemis explains she has to hunt down her stepmother, Hera, in order to get Evan back into Zeus's good graces, Evan demands to accompany her. However, the journey turns out to be a test that could bring them closer together or tear them apart forever.

CHAPTER ONE

5 *14 AD*

Artemis crept through the darkening forest, her bare feet barely making a sound as she hunted her prey. The scent of damp earth and spring wildflowers filled the air. The *thump*, *thump* of her heartbeat and that of the deer hiding amongst the foliage a few feet away were the only sounds.

The doe's head rose above the brush, her ears flickered as she carefully stepped forward. Artemis stilled, slowly pulled an arrow from her quiver and drew her bow. Before she could fire, the animal jerked her head toward Artemis, then took off in the opposite direction.

Damn. So close.

A familiar, masculine scent mixed with that of forest

and earth met her nose. Annoyance bathed her, turning to anger as she twisted sharply to face the intruder. Evangelos, minor god of the messengers, stood a few feet away, his own bow at the ready. She snarled, glancing from the bow to the smug look on his face. "I thought Hermes taught his sons better manners. Don't you know it is dangerous to sneak up on me during a hunt?"

One large, bare shoulder rose in a lazy shrug as he stalked closer. She planted her feet in place, refusing to show him any type of weakness—he would never know how her body heated when he was near, something she hadn't experienced with any other man.

She was a pure goddess, untouched by the desires of the flesh, and she would stay that way. Not even Evangelos could change who she was or her nature.

He stopped a foot away, the heat from his virile body reaching out to her, coaxing her to come closer. "I want you to teach me to hunt."

Steeling her spine, she narrowed her gaze at him. "You can already hunt."

"Not like you. I want you to show me your way."

"Why?"

He took a step nearer. She desperately wanted to move away, but giving up ground would be a sign of weakness. "Does the reason matter?"

No, it didn't matter. She couldn't care less why he wanted her to teach him. "What do you offer me in return?" He had to know asking a boon of her meant she'd require some sort of payment in exchange.

One corner of his mouth lifted, drawing her attention to his full lips. What was wrong with her? She must be ill. It was the only reasonable explanation for her reaction to him. When he spoke, his tone softened, almost to a whisper. "I offer my services to you during the time it takes you to teach me."

Suspicion crawled up her spine. "What services?"

He closed the distance between them until only a breath separated them. "Anything you wish, my goddess."

She was fully unprepared for what happened next. When his soft lips brushed hers, every nerve in her body lit up as if charged by lightning. For a moment she allowed his testing caress, but when he wrapped an arm around her waist, she broke the kiss and slapped him. The sound of the strike echoed off the trees as his head whipped to the side, thunder to emphasize the storm he'd awakened with his touch.

"Do that again and I'll kill you," she warned.

DESPITE REJECTING HIS ADVANCE, Artemis trained Evangelos. By the third day after their first exchange, she discovered he didn't need her tutelage. However, by then, it was too late—she'd looked forward to their time together each day. They shared many interests and, best of all, he loved the hunt as much as she did.

She'd allowed him to steal another kiss the day before and found she liked the desire he awakened within her. Although she worried she would become addicted to his touch and long for more, she also began to wonder if it would it be so bad to have him as her consort.

For the first time in her life, she considered taking a lover. Evangelos stirred feeling inside her she'd never known, never dreamed of experiencing. She felt alive with him, and found a fulfillment unlike anything else.

The energy in the air electrified. She smiled and turned to the terrace of her temple. His back faced her, but that didn't stop her from crossing the space between them. When she stepped out on the terrace, his sadness hit her like a thick wave. Her heart sank as fury started to build. She'd been a fool.

Before she could speak, he glanced at her over his shoulder. "I've been lying to you."

Guilt replaced her sadness, making her sigh in relief. "I know. I've known for four days."

"And yet you let me feel guilty about it?" He faced her, brows drawn.

She bit her lower lip to keep from laughing. He was cute distressed. "You weren't all that remorseful until tonight. What has changed?"

Glancing away, he shook his head. "I...I'm falling

in love with you and need to be honest with my intentions."

Her stomach whirled and, for the first time in her long existence, she didn't know how to handle the situation. "I'm not sure…"

Closing the gap between them, he took her hands in his. "I don't care if we have to keep it a secret. I want you, I have wanted you for a long time."

"You're a deceitful man, Evangelos," she teased

His lips twitched. "You bring my best qualities out, milady."

She leaned in and pressed her lips to his. "The thought of not being your friend makes my heart ache. To others that is all it can be, for now."

He wrapped his arms around her, picking her up and twirling her around. "I'll take you any way I can."

"Shut up and kiss me again."

CHAPTER TWO

P resent Day

A SINGLE TEAR rolled down Artemis's cheek as she gazed into the looking pool outside her home in Olympus. The crystal clear water allowed her to watch over her daughter while she visited the human world. Artemis had never used it to seek *him* out. Then again, until recently, she believed Evangelos—her one true love and Ashlynn's father—to be dead and beyond even her powers of sight.

Her chest tightened as she recalled the day her father told her Evan had died. Meant to be the happiest day of her life, the day became the worst in only a matter of moments.

The moment she woke, she knew something to be

amiss. Springing from her bed, she'd conjured her chiton to hide her nudity before she set out in search of Evangelos. When she reached his home, he was not there. An odd sadness filled her, and she decided to go see her father. The closer to Zeus's palace she got, the stronger the sick feeling of dread grew. She entered the large mansion and sought out her father. "Zeus."

"What is it?" The god king boomed from the top of the stairs.

"Have you seen Evangelos?"

Her father studied her as he descended the stairs, his face devoid of emotion. Her stomach knotted and a lump formed in her throat. "I'm afraid Evangelos is no longer with us."

"No. No. How?" She shook her head and stumbled backwards. Her father stared, his brows dipping and his eyes dulled with pity. Tears streamed down her cheeks and she turned and ran to her own palace where she dropped to her knees beside the looking pool, her palm flattened over her belly. As if her hand could protect the child who would never meet his or her father.

More tears rolled down her cheeks as the memory faded. She hated the weakness she allowed herself to fall into. With a wave of one hand over the water, Evan appeared at his place of employment. Ashlynn mentioned he labored as a mechanic, fixing human vehicles. Seeing him alive made her heart ache all the more. How did she not know of the deception sooner? Footsteps from across the garden drew her attention.

Zeus stopped a few feet from the pond, long silver hair cascading over his shoulders. She stood and turned her back to him, but stilled as he spoke. "Please stay."

Without facing him, she answered quietly, "I have nothing to say to you."

"Artemis, you can't hold a grudge forever."

"I have managed to do so for over fifteen hundred years."

He sighed. "I've come to ask a favor of you."

She laughed, although she felt no humor. "Why would I do anything for you?"

He fell silent for several long moments, drawing her curiosity. Glancing over her shoulder at him, she saw something the god king never allowed anyone to see—weakness. Pain and sorrow etched his features and darkened his eyes. When he met her gaze, he stepped forward. She quickly turned away, but didn't run inside like she wanted.

"In exchange for this favor, I'll reinstate Evangelos as a god of messengers."

Her heart stopped for two beats. Could he be telling the truth? It wasn't above or below Zeus to use words against others, to promise them anything to get what he wanted, yet fail to deliver. "How do I know you'll keep your word?" She straightened her spine even as another tear fell down her cheek. She couldn't go to Evan with false hopes. Somehow she knew deep in her core he wouldn't want her in his current state. He was too emotionally damaged from what her father had done to him.

The rustle of Zeus's robes indicated he advanced closer, but still she didn't turn to face him. "I've carried the guilt for too long. I believed you'd get over him, that the thing between you two was nothing."

She whirled around, her sadness hardening to a cold rage. "*Nothing?* You thought it was nothing? I loved him. I carried his child alone and mourned his death, all because of your lies."

Zeus's eyes widened and he held his palms out. "Artemis, put your bow away. You do not wish me harm."

"Do not tell me what I wish." Artemis stepped forward, forcing him to back up. "You took my heart away, destroyed everything."

Much too fast for her to track with the blind rage coursing inside her, Zeus disarmed her and held her in a tight hug. "I am sorry for the misunderstanding." She wiggled to break free, but he tightened his grip. "Deliver a message to Hera for me. I'll return Evangelos's god status and give my blessing to your wedding, if you choose it. I give my word to you, as a god of fate."

As his words sank in, she sagged against him. "Hera hates me. She'd kill me as soon as I got close to her."

He stroked her hair from her forehead. "She doesn't hate you. She hates your mother."

"Okay, she doesn't like me. How am I supposed to deliver a message to her? Do you even know where she is?" Artemis extracted herself from his arms and straightened her knee-length gown as she studied him.

His brows drew together, forming a single line over his eyes. "We are fighting. This is the hundredth day without her. I've searched for her, but she is blocking my attempts."

"Wow, sounds serious. What did you do this time?"

He narrowed his eyes, opened his mouth, and then closed it again before saying, "It doesn't matter." A small white envelope materialized between his fingers. "Do not open it, or the deal is off. This is for my wife's eyes only."

Without another word or waiting for her reply, he dematerialized. She stared down at the envelope and frowned. Never had she remotely cared where Hera ran off to during one of hers and Zeus's "falling outs." Where in Hades was she going to find the queen of gods?

EVAN TURNED the ratchet a little too hard, breaking the bolt off. His knuckles slammed into the engine. "Fuck. Sonofabitch." Not bothering to wipe away the blood, he tossed the ratchet into his toolbox and stormed into his office. By the time he reached the bathroom, the cuts across the backs of his fingers had already healed.

No, Evan wasn't human. He wasn't a god either, forever stuck in the human world with limited powers.

Yet he was stronger, faster, and a hell of a lot older than the mortals surrounding him. Voices on the other side of the door made him pause with his hands under the running water. Turning off the faucet, he grabbed a hand towel and yanked the door open. His heart stopped for a brief moment at the sight of the woman standing in the middle of his office.

Long red hair cascaded over her shoulders, silky and vibrant against the light green dress she wore. Scanning up her body to her face, he met her haunted green stare. *Damn.* Her beauty stunned him, even more radiant in the flesh than his imagination remembered. Her gaze dropped to his towel-wrapped hand and she frowned. "You're hurt."

When she stepped forward, he backed away. "I'm fine." Glancing at one of his mechanics, Evan nodded toward the door. "See if you can get the bolt shaft out of the head for me?" The other man nodded and left the office. Evan unwrapped his hand and threw the towel in the small laundry basket inside the bathroom. "Why are you here, Artemis?"

He swore her bottom lip trembled before she turned away to look out the window. "I've bargained with Zeus to reinstate your godhood."

"What?"

She cast a sharp glare over her shoulder. "You heard me. I came to let you know."

Her sudden change of mood told him he'd hurt her with his cold words. *Fuck.* "Artemis…" She dematerialized before he could finish. Raking a hand through his hair, he fought the impulse to scream, to curse the god king for banishing him to the human world in a jealous rage. One hasty decision by Zeus destroyed his life and ripped the only woman he'd ever loved away from him. He withdrew his cell from his pocket and called Ash. She answered on the first ring. "Your mother left here a few moments ago. She's upset."

Ash released a heavy sigh. "I'll talk to her. Keep in mind, she's lived the past fifteen hundred years grieving your death."

She hung up on him. *Good one, asshole.*

CHAPTER THREE

Artemis sat on a stone bench in the rose gardens outside the dragons' home—her daughter's new home with her mate, Tyson. Tears blurred her vision and her nose tingled, fueling her anger at herself for daring to believe for even an instant that things could be as they once were. Evan didn't want her, not after so much time had passed. She was going on Zeus's mission, regardless— deliver his message then return home, alone.

She sensed her daughter before she entered the small courtyard. "I saw Evangelos."

"I know. He called."

"He didn't want me there." Although she tried to contain the storm of emotions within, some of her misery leaked out in her tone, frustrating her further. It was bad enough that she ached from a rejection she should have foreseen. She should have better control than to let others, even her daughter, know of her weakness, and finding she didn't was humbling.

Ashlynn appeared in front of her as she knelt down and took her hands. "That is not true. He's hurting, like you. Men handle feelings different than we do."

After a few moments, Artemis squared her shoulders. "I have to find Hera."

"What? Why?"

She met her daughter's concerned stare. "I have to deliver a message to her for Zeus. In exchange, Evangelos gets reinstated as a god."

Ashlynn stood, folded her arms, and narrowed her eyes. "If you live through it. Do you even know where she is?"

"No, but I must find her."

"Not alone, you aren't." The masculine voice behind her attracted her attention and Artemis jumped to her feet and whirled around to glare at Evangelos, standing a few feet away. Annoyance made her blood run cold. "You have no right to tell me what to do."

He stepped forward, but Artemis held her ground. "Why do you get to choose how I get my godhood back? How do you know I even *want* it back?"

Artemis drew back, shocked. How could he not want to return home? Return to her? Pain gripped her heart like a vise, making it difficult to grasp what he tried to tell her. Had he moved on? A lump lodged in her throat.

After a moment, she turned away. "I see."

His thick, strong arms encircled her, squeezing her tight against him. "Please don't teleport away from this argument."

The growl in his voice mixed with his familiar cedar scent was her undoing. It'd been too long since she'd been held by him. Turning toward him, she cupped his face. "I've spent the last millennia and a half believing you were dead, never seeing your smile, never hearing your voice. Now that I've found you, it would be unbearable for me to let you go again."

He stared at her for a brief moment before crushing his lips to hers. Sliding her hands to his nape, she pressed her body to his and opened when he swiped his tongue along the seam of her lips. Tingles skittered over his skin, intensifying her mounting desire.

Artemis broke the kiss. She released a sigh as she rested her head against his chest. "I need to find Hera."

"I'm going with you. No arguing."

Lifting her head, she gazed into his emerald eyes. "I'm not sure where to find her."

A sensual, yet wicked smile formed on his handsome face. "I bet our daughter knows, or at least can find out for us."

They looked to Ash, who rolled her eyes. "Come inside. Markus might know."

Artemis stepped out of Evan's embrace to follow Ash down the stone walkway into the house. Silently, Evan fell in step beside her. She could still feel his uneasiness, it radiated off him in waves of brittle tension. She couldn't tell if it was the mission or being around her that put him on edge, nor could she find the words to ask.

Once inside the large foyer, Ty greeted them with a nod before he hooked an arm around his mate's waist and kissed her. Ash flattened a hand on his chest. "We need to talk with Markus."

"He's in the great room." Ty motioned them straight ahead.

Entering the great room, Artemis's gaze fell on Markus, who lounged on the sofa with Gwen snuggled into his side. His fingers twisted a strand of her blonde hair and both looked calm and peaceful. Their bond twined around them in a beautiful hue of blue and silver glow only the gods and a few other magic born creatures could see.

Markus met her gaze and started to move, but Artemis held up her hand. "No need to get up. I need to find Hera."

He raised a brow. "May I ask why?"

"I need to deliver a message for Zeus."

Silence fell around them as Markus glanced between her and Evan. With a heavy sigh, he nodded. "Ares!"

Artemis's heart thumped rapidly. She didn't particularly care for her half-brother any more than she cared for Hera. At least the god of war didn't try to kill her, something she'd come to expect from the god queen. When Ares materialized, she squared her shoulders and asked him where his mother hid.

Ares pressed his lips together in a thin line. After a long moment, he answered. "I heard she makes appearances at Zeus's temple in Athens regularly."

"What are the chances she'll be there?"

He shrugged, appearing bored with the conversation. "By now, she likely knows you will be searching for her, so she'll probably make a game out of it."

Swallowing the dread lodged in her throat, she pushed down the fear she refused to show anyone. "What kind of game?"

"My guess is anything she must do to ensure you fail." A wicked, deadly smile formed on the god's face seconds before he dematerialized.

Frustration made her want to scream. Ares didn't answer any of her questions, not outright. She faced Evan. "Now what?"

"We go to Athens. If she truly is ready to make a game out of it, then we'll play."

Her fury with the whole thing melted away, replaced by the desire to hunt down the god queen. It was just too bad she couldn't put one of her arrows through Hera's heart in the end. "Okay. Let's hunt ourselves a goddess."

Evan framed her face and kissed her quick. "Gods, you're beautiful. I've been so angry for so long."

She smiled as her cheeks heated. "Take me to your home. I want to know what happened. Everything."

With a nod, he glanced to Ash, making Artemis follow his gaze. Her daughter waved them off. "Go. But be careful."

Artemis laughed and stepped closer to Ash. "It was I who said those same words to you, not so very long ago."

Movement behind her daughter made Artemis smile. Tyson moved in like a predator, snaking his arms around his mate to tug her close. "You know your daughter is as stubborn as you are."

Rolling her eyes, the goddess turned to offer Evan her hand. He linked their fingers together, but before they teleported away, Ty called her name. "If you need anything, you can summon me or Ash."

Her heart warmed. "Thank you."

She gave a nod to Evan and the world dissolved around her as she flashed to his home in Georgia. Standing in his living room, she scanned her surroundings. Dark hardwood floors stretched through the house. Hunter green curtains contrasted nicely with the white walls. Inhaling deeply, she almost groaned at the masculine scent of Evan in the air. Gods, she'd missed his scent.

"Artemis?"

She faced him and drew her brows together. "Yes?"

One side of his mouth lifted. "I need to make dinner. What do you like to eat?"

She frowned, not knowing what kinds of mortal foods she liked. The gods didn't worry about meals unless it was a celebration or some other type of gathering. Artemis never found any reason to stay in the mortal world for extended periods of time prior to this occasion—not since she'd learned of his death and lost the desire to hunt for pleasure. "I'm not sure."

His crooked smile faded. "Sorry, I guess I'm used to being around humans."

When he turned away and disappeared into another room, she dropped her shoulders. His brief sadness made her feel guilty, even though none of it was her fault. She couldn't stop wondering what would have happened if she'd searched for him. Could she have found him?

Hesitantly, she followed him and realized the other room was a kitchen. Evan's back was to her as he poured a red sauce into a pot. "Sorry."

He spun around, his brows knitted together. "You have nothing to be sorry for. Ever since Ash came into my life a few months ago, I've reevaluated my anger and redirected it to the right person—or god, in this case." His features softened and he held out his hand. When she took it, he tugged her forward, knocking her off balance. She tumbled into him, laughter bursting from her as he held her tight against him. His warmth enveloped her, soothing her worries away. The casual embrace also raised the muted desire she'd always had for him.

Kissing her nose, Evan pulled back to meet her gaze for a long moment before releasing her and stepping away. She shivered at the absence of his body heat. "Tell me what happened."

He turned back to her holding a spoon with the red sauce on it. "Taste this."

Doing as he'd asked, she opened and allowed him the guide the spoon into her mouth. Her taste buds burst to life with the combined flavors of tomatoes and herbs she couldn't name. "It's good."

"I'm glad you like it. It goes over pasta." He smiled, then his eyes widened as if an idea came to him. "I have something else I think you'll like. I'll be back."

He rushed through a doorway a few feet from where they stood. Moments later, he emerged with a wine bottle in one hand and two stemmed glasses in the other. "I have had wine before."

"Yes, but how long has it been since you had red wine from Ikaria?"

Interest lit up within her and she reached for the bottle, but Evan kept it out of reach. An island in the Aegean Sea, just off the shores Greece, Ikaria was known for their strong red wine. Folding her arms, she glared at him. "Don't tease, Evangelos."

His brows bunched together before he focused on pouring the wine. "I never tease, Art." He handed her a glass. When she gripped the stem, he held onto it and added, "Call me Evan. I'm not the same person I used to be."

Her heart skipped a beat as she studied him closely. Small lines fanned out from the corners of his eyes, making him look older. There was a touch of grey in his temples. Butterflies swarmed in her belly. Had he aged? "Are you no longer immortal?"

She reached up to touch the tiny silver hairs and he leaned his face into her palm. "I am. The gray is so I fit in with the humans. Part of the curse is that I'm to live in the mortal world for the rest of my very long existence. I've been able to perform magic for centuries now. No, longer than that...."

"What is it?'

"Ash is 1500 year old?"

"Fifteen, twenty, why?"

He started to laugh and picked up his glass. "It all makes sense now." His green gaze met hers. "I'll explain everything I know. Go make yourself comfortable in the living room. I'll be out shortly with dinner."

Dread and a hint of fear ran in her veins, but she did as he asked. When she dropped on the sofa, she sipped her wine, allowing the rich notes of berry and vanilla linger on her tongue before swallowing. Cradling the glass in her hands, she tried to keep her anger toward her father to a simmer.

Zeus would answer to her for everything he'd done to Evan, a promise she'd be glad to keep.

EVAN CARRIED the tray with their plates and his wine into the living room. He couldn't help but remember the day Zeus tracked him down and sentenced him to life on

Earth. The god king's words made no sense at the time, but now—knowing he had a daughter—clarity gave him hope.

Artemis sat on the sofa, long legs crossed and one foot shaking vigorously. *What in Hades has her annoyed*? "Art? Are you okay?"

She snapped her attention to him. "Please tell me what Zeus did to you. I can't take the suspense any longer."

With a sigh, he set the tray on the coffee table. "I will. I need to think on where to start."

"How about the day you left?"

He nodded. "Okay. It was early morning. I planned to surprise you…" He paused and stared into her pale green eyes. His heart skipped a beat as the image of her —much like it was in that moment—appeared in his mind. "How did I not know?"

Her shoulders dropped and she relaxed a little. "When I woke, I knew. I looked for you, but by the time I found Zeus, he said you were no longer with us. My heart shattered."

The tears filling her eyes undid him. He grabbed her into a tight hug. "Zeus believed I was sleeping with Hera and cursed me. No questions, no trial. He just spoke the words and I was sent here."

"What were the words he used?" Her voice trembled, as if she wasn't sure she wanted to know.

"He said, 'Evangelos, I banish you to the mortal realm where you will live without magic until your first-born turns one thousand years old.'" Saying the words aloud made him feel more like an idiot.

Artemis opened her mouth, then closed it. She tapped her glass with a nail and took a deep breath. "You've been able to come home for over five hundred years."

Taking the glass from her before she shattered it, he set it on the table then cupped her face. "I didn't know about Ash, but Zeus must've known."

She jerked out of his grasp, stood, and begun to pace. "But he didn't know until I found him and asked about you." The anger lines under her eyes softened as if she remembered something. "For a brief moment, I sensed his guilt as he spoke of your death. I was so overcome with grief, though, I dismissed any signals he may have tried to send me."

"What are you going to do?" He feared she'd do something like kill her father, which would fracture the thin veils between the worlds.

"I'm going to give the message back to him and tell him where to shove it."

Evan jumped up and gripped her arms. "Don't. Think about it. No matter how much of an ass Zeus can be, he is king and always has a reason behind his madness. I think this is a test."

"What kind of test? Why would I need to be tested? I'm his daughter. He should know I'm loyal." Her lips set in a thin line and her eyes darkened.

"He not testing you, but me. If I go back to Olympus

now, I'll be run out. I have to prove I still belong there." He waited and watched how she focused on his face, thinking about what he'd said.

Several long moments passed before she let go of her anger and nodded. "So, what now? We go ahead with this mission?"

"Yes, as he intended."

"Where do we begin?"

"Tomorrow, we go to the Temple of Olympian Zeus in Athens."

Artemis pursed her lips and tapped her foot. "She won't be there."

Evan smiled. "No, but if she is in on Zeus's plan, she'll leave us a clue."

CHAPTER FOUR

E van belonged to her. Artemis would do anything to have him back in her life, in her bed, including going on the crazy hunt the god king and queen mapped out for them. Well, at least she knew Zeus was behind the journey. Knowing Hera, she'd do anything to make Artemis suffer.

They didn't call Artemis the goddess of the hunt for nothing. If it was a chase the queen wanted, she'd get it, but on Artemis's terms. "We do this my way. It is no secret my stepmother doesn't like me. If she is indeed part of this test, then she'll set up obstacles along the way."

A wicked smile formed on Evan's lips. "Agreed. We'll be ready for them."

"We'll have to be careful about teleporting."

"So we leave when it is early morning in Greece, less chance to pop in when tourist are around." Evan turned, picked up her glass and handed it to her. "Come, eat. There are things I've only dreamt of doing to you while we were apart."

Her skin flushed and she almost told him to screw the meal, but she was in the human realm and needed the substance.

As soon as she finished her spaghetti, he cleaned the dishes while she drank her wine. Her belly was full and her head spun from the alcohol, but she felt great. Her earlier nervousness over their pending journey dulled.

Footsteps sounded behind her a moment before Evan slipped his arms around her shoulders over the back of the couch. "Are you ready for bed?"

"I'm not tired," she teased.

He bit her ear lobe, drawing a squeak from her. In an instant, she was on her back in the middle of his large bed. His mouth covered hers, crushing her lips. When he licked the seam of her mouth, she opened, allowing him entry. A soft moan rumbled up her throat as pleasure rushed through her veins and crawled over her skin.

By the will of her mind, she stripped them both and sucked in a sharp breath at the electric current flowing between them when their skin touched. Their powers reached out to one another, knowing each strength and weakness of the other.

Tingles raced over her, bouncing pleasure from Evan to her and vice-versa. Gods, it felt amazing to be bared to him, touching him and being touched by him again.

He broke the kiss, teased her jaw with his teeth and

continued to nip his way to her throat and lower. When he closed his mouth over one breast, she nearly jumped off the bed. The unexpected surge of pleasure seemed stronger than she'd remembered.

Her pussy pulsated, begging for his cock. She let out a whimper and rotated her hips against him. When he rose above her, she reached for him, but he grabbed her wrist with one hand and held it in place above her head. She smiled and raised a brow. "What will you do with me now?"

He didn't smile back, but she saw wickedness in the green depths of his eyes. "I'm going to eat your pussy until you scream."

Good gods. What in Hades was he waiting on?

When he pressed his lips to her belly, she bit her lip to keep a cry from escaping. Heat spread from his kiss down to her core.

He lifted his head to meet her stare. "Don't move those hands."

Releasing her wrist, he slid down her body to lay between her legs. She was tempted to disobey him to see what he'd do, but she wanted his mouth on her too badly. There was plenty of time to misbehave later.

With his index finger, he circled her clit before he traced between her folds. Desire made her head swim. When he entered her with the finger, she gasped and lifted her hips. He covered her clit with his mouth and sucked as he slid another finger inside her and pumped.

She fisted the sheets and moved her hips in time

with each lick. Her body grew more and more sensitive as he thrust his fingers in and out while his tongue teased and licked. Pleasure built, overriding her ability to think or to hold back the orgasm from crashing over her.

A scream ripped from her throat as she came. He gave a final lick as the last shuddering wave rolled through her before he crawled up her body.

Hovering over her, he stared at her with a grin plastered on his face. "You're beautiful when you come."

"So are you, if I remember correctly."

"Well, your memory is about to refreshed, goddess."

Her stomach flipped, firing up her desire for this man. *No, not man. God.* He would always be her god, not matter the outcome of their mission.

Looping his larger arms under her knees, he thrust into her, filling her over and over. Pleasure rolled through her core and spread to every fiber of her being. Evan moved his hands to hold her ankles and he continued to move in and out, picking up speed with each thrust until his body tensed. She cried out as the climax hit her. His orgasm came shortly after.

He collapsed beside her, pulling her face to his so he could claim her mouth. She sighed and snuggled into him. "That was amazing."

"Yes. Give me five minutes and we'll take a shower."

She laughed. "I don't know. I like having your scent all over me."

He nipped her shoulder and she shuddered. "Believe me, you will wear my scent every day for all eternity."

She frowned and rolled to her side to face him. "When this…test…or whatever it is, is over, we'll talk about it. I need to make sure I survive Hera."

"You will survive. I'll make sure if it."

He rose above her and cupped her cheek. "How about that shower now?"

Smiling, she settled her cheek into his palm. "Sounds great, but that's it. Shower, then sleep. I have a feeling we have a long day ahead of us."

"Deal," he answered before kissing her forehead.

CHAPTER FIVE

Light filtered through the blinds of Evan's bedroom. At first he thought everything that happened the day before was a dream. *A wonderful dream.*

Then Artemis stirred and snuggled into him. A smile lifted his lips and his heart thumped rapidly behind his ribs. With a sigh, he ran his fingers through her long red hair. *It's real.* He had her in his bed and made love to her multiple times during the night and morning.

Glancing at the clock, he groaned at the time—four o'clock in the afternoon. They'd slept the day away. Well, in between bouts of outstanding sex. He nudged Artemis. "Art, time to get up."

She yawned and opened her eyes. "What time is it?"

"Four o'clock, or eleven PM in Athens."

"Great. The temple shouldn't be occupied." She snuggled into him. "Mmm. Do we have to move?"

He kissed the top of her head, inhaling her clean, earthy scent. "As much as I don't want to, I'm afraid we must."

The sooner they found Hera and delivered the message—if there was a message—the sooner he could make Artemis his.

With a dramatic sigh, she rose from bed and conjured a white and green sundress to cover her body. She faced him and smiled as she ran her fingers through her hair, magically combing the red, silken strands smooth. "I'm ready."

He laughed and reached for her, but she darted out of reach. "Oh no. We need to be going. If I get back in bed, I'm not coming out."

So tempting. He teleported to stand behind her and brushed her hair aside to kiss her neck. "I want you in my bed every night."

She shivered under his touch and pride swelled inside him. A month ago, before Ash came to him and Ty not-so-gently persuaded him to stop being an ass, he would have turned Artemis away. His bitter anger toward the gods consumed him to the point where reason wasn't an option.

In a way, he owed Ty a fucking beer or something for pulling his head out of his ass because his heart was the goddess in his arms. He'd never be able to let her go again and wasn't sure how he'd survived losing her the first time.

Willing a pair of jeans and t-shirt to cover his nudity, he asked, "Are you ready?"

When she nodded, they teleported to Athens, Greece.

As they materialized in the main hall of the temple, Evan shook his head in amazement. "I thought the temple was in ruins."

"It is. This is an illusion. Hera does it when she visits, which tells me she's been here recently." Artemis glanced around the temple.

Evan also scanned the area, frustration mounting, until he spied a small table tucked in the corner to the right of the large statue of Zeus seated on his throne.

"There." He pointed and advanced toward it.

Upon closer inspection, he realized it wasn't a table, as he'd first thought, but a hip high, column-like plant stand. A bottle of wine rested on the top, alongside a map of the Aegean Islands. He glanced to Artemis and shook his head. "She's not very subtle."

Artemis shrugged. "She never was. If she had an issue with you, she'd either kill you or curse you. Subtle was never part of her nature." She picked up the bottle of wine. "I guess we're going to Ikaria." Evan gripped her elbow, but she shook her head. "Let's take a boat in the morning. No need to be so eager. Plus there is a little shop I want to visit before we leave."

"Okay. What shall we do until then?"

Her green eyes sparkled and the corners of her lips

lifted. "See Athens. It's been ages since I've been in the city."

Snaking an arm around her waist, he tugged her flush against him. "I know a place with light music and great food."

"Sounds amazing." She nipped at his bottom lip.

He groaned. "You keep that up, and we'll be ordering room service in the nearest hotel."

She shoved at him. "Oh no. You promised music *and* food."

Laughing, he laced his fingers with hers and tugged her out of the temple. For the first time since his banishment, he felt alive. His hopes for the future returned. He hoped Artemis was part of his future.

ARTEMIS TAPPED her foot and swayed to the music. The small tavern Evan selected was perfect. Only about a dozen humans scattered about the room, enjoying the ambiance and entertainment. A few of the older ones glanced her way every so often and she wondered if they recognized her. If they did, they didn't say anything, just glanced her way and then returned to their own amusements. Leaning into Evan, she asked, "How did you know about this place?"

He held up his cell phone, a smirk forming on his sinfully sweet lips. "Ash suggested it."

"Of course." Artemis hid a smile behind her cup

before she sipped her tea. "Our daughter is playing matchmaker."

One corner of his mouth lifted and he stretched an arm around her shoulders. "Should I tell her it's no use?"

"No. Let her have her fun."

"Let who have fun?"

Artemis jerked at Ashlynn's voice. Her daughter sat at a nearby table with her dragon mate. "What are you doing here?"

With a wave of a hand, Ash stood and dragged her chair over to join them. "Ty and I arrived a few moments ago. There is no way I'm going to allow you to do this on your own."

Folding her arms, Artemis glared at her daughter. "This is not your mission, it is a test for Evan and me."

"I know, I know, Zeus's twisted way to bring the two of you back together. Yet, if it wasn't for the Oracle 'misplacing' Evan's ledger, I wouldn't have found him. If I hadn't, I wonder if my dear old grandfather would have said anything to you." Ash narrowed her eyes as she scanned the restaurant. "Forgive me if I don't trust the king and queen."

All valid points Artemis turned over and over in her mind since making the bargain with Zeus. *But, still...* "We don't either, but we can make a vacation of it and enjoy the journey."

Ash laughed, but it was Ty who spoke. "All the more reason we need to be here to watch your back.

While you two are honeymooning, Ash and I can be on the lookout for Hera's traps."

Studying the dragon, Artemis wished he'd take his damned sunglasses off so she could see his eyes. She never really cared for dragons much. It wasn't like she despised them, she'd simply never had any use for them. They were her half-brother's creation, not hers. Yet, Ty proved himself to be a strong and loyal mate to her daughter.

"We aren't honeymooning."

Ash laughed again and this time almost fell out of her chair, making the dragon smile as well. "*Mitera*, please, don't make jokes. Why do you think we didn't go with you when you left the mansion? We gave you time to take care of the sexual tension first. If I had to listen to the two of you having…"

"Ashlynn!" Embarrassed, Artemis turned away from her daughter and glanced around to make sure no one overheard the conversation.

Evan patted her arm. "Ash, don't tease your mother."

Ash sighed. "Fine. Sorry, Ma, but we are here to help."

Ty leaned forward in his chair to whisper, "I was able to get some information from Ares about his mother's intentions. Of course, he didn't know the details, but he did say she wouldn't make your journey an easy one. Ares said he saw Hera talking with Karin."

Dread scorched her insides. Karin—a deadly and

mentally unstable, vampire-like daemon—was imprisoned in Tartarus as far as Artemis knew. "She's imprisoned."

"That's what I said. My father only shrugged and said this was the queen of gods." Ty worked his jaw. Artemis wasn't sure if it was because he was pissed at Ares or Hera, though it seemed likely both shared his anathema.

Evan growled beside her. "There is no telling what Hera has over the daemon. We'll have to prepare for Karin popping in at any time."

Artemis nodded. *But how did you prepare for a vampire attack?*

CHAPTER SIX

Evan inhaled the salty, sea air as the yacht they'd rented glided across the water. The slight rocking made him dizzy, but at least he hadn't got sick. *Yet.*

Artemis walked up behind him, sliding her hand under his shirt and up his back. Need filled his cock and spread throughout his body in a hot wave threatening to drown him. Reaching back, he took her hand and pulled her around so her front pressed to his. Her pale green eyes sparkled with wicked desire.

Dipping his head, he kissed her soft and quick on the lips. She melted into him, but he could sense her temper. "Karin may be insane, but I believe we can reason with her."

Artemis gazed up at him, eyes narrowing. "You can't reason with crazy."

He chuckled. "No, but you can offer it what it wants and make an ally of it."

"Okay, I'll bite. How do you propose we do that?"

"We find out what Hera offered her or is holding over her and propose our own deal." He paused to let her think about it. She studied him for a few moments, then turned in his arms to press her back to his front.

"I'm not sure we have anything of value to give her."

He kissed her temple. "We have to try."

"What if she can't be tempted to join us?"

"Then we'll have to kill her." Her back straightened and he felt a hint of excitement drift off her. A smile tugged at his lips. His huntress loved a good fight.

Running a finger down her cheek, over her jaw, and down to her collarbone, he whispered, "Let's stop talking about things we can't control and go find some privacy."

She whirled around to stare him in the eyes. "Where?"

"It is a yacht. There's a bedroom below."

Her eyes brightened, then darkened with hunger right before she pivoted and tugged him toward the berth. They got a few yards from the door when a woman materialized in front of them. Her eyes matched her hair, both dark as night. When the woman—*no, vampire*—smiled a humorless smile, her small, lethal fangs elongated.

Out of instinct, Evan stepped in front of Artemis with his hands in fists at his sides. "Karin."

She tilted her head slightly as she studied him. Her

black eyes narrowed and she stepped forward. Behind him, Artemis fought his attempt to block her from the vampire's view. The goddess managed to get around him and held her hands up to the female. "What has Hera offered you?"

Karin laughed. "The god queen makes promises she can't keep. Or won't keep."

Her words didn't make sense. Evan placed a hand on Artemis's arm. "Then why are you working with her?"

With a low growl, the vampire pointed at him. "I obey only one god. Queen or not, she doesn't own me."

Artemis relaxed next him and laced her fingers with his. "So, why are you here?"

"To warn you. I wasn't the only distraction Hera planned."

"I'm not surprised." Artemis snorted. "In fact, I'd be disappointed if you were."

He shifted back and forth beside her, growing more anxious by the moment. "Why would you help us?"

The vamp darted her gaze to him and snarled, "Because I don't like the queen bitch."

Artemis touched his arm, trying to calm him so to avoid upsetting the unstable female. "Who do you work for?"

"Hades. He is the only one I obey."

"Did he send you?"

She smiled. "He said to keep an eye on Hera and to help the dragons."

Glancing at Evan then to Ty as he stepped up next to them, Artemis tensed and glared at Karin. "What are you talking about?"

Beside them, Ty let out a low growl. It was hard for Evan to gauge the dragon's reaction due to the ever-present sunglasses he wore, he could sense a growing annoyance since Karin showed.

"Help us how?" Ty asked, drawing Karin's attention.

She tilted her head and frowned. "Gary is a bad dragon. I don't like him. Hades says to go to Markus after I see that the goddess of the hunt completes her test."

The vampire's rambling was a little hard to follow. When Artemis opened her mouth to ask another question, the boat rocked to the side. Evan reached out and grabbed her arms to steady her. Karin hissed and ran to the side railing only to be thrown back a few feet.

"Fucking daemons." Ty formed a softball size fireball and threw it at the daemon crawling over the railing. The creature screamed as fire engulfed him, turning him into ash.

Evan whirled around at the sound of footsteps and met his daughter's narrowed-eyed glare. Artemis too turned and he could tell mother and daughter were sharing a thought or two. Together they conjured their bows and arrows, aimed and fired at a couple of daemons. The arrows hit their targets through the hearts, killing them instantly.

More daemons materialized on the deck, too many

for the five of them to fight off. Beside him, Artemis closed her eyes and raised her hands to the sky. The squawk of seagulls and other birds sounded in the distance, drawing closer. Evan smiled. The goddess had called out to the animals.

Suddenly Ty shifted into his dragon in a flash of red and gold. He wings stretched out wide and he took to the air. The large dragon hovered a few feet over the yacht, staring down at Artemis as if waiting for her command. The smoke rolling from his nostrils told Evan he wasn't happy about it.

Artemis gasped, then cursed. "Shit. Sorry, Ty. I didn't mean..."

Ash touched her arm. "He knows. Let him go so he can do want he was made to do."

Lips lifting into a satisfied smile, Artemis waved a hand in the air, breaking the connection she had with the dragon. Ty dived toward the boat, scooping up several daemons in his mouth, gathered the rest in his claws and flew off.

Karin clapped. "He's going to rip them apart with his claws and teeth!"

Artemis sighed and Ash crunched up her face. "Thanks for the visual, Karin."

"You're welcome."

Ash glanced at Artemis and rolled her eyes. "The vamp is crazy."

"Yeah, but I'm glad she's on our side." Evan said as

he wrapped his arms around Artemis's waist from behind.

She sighed and leaned into him. He was glad the vamp appeared to be on their side as well, although he wasn't sure if they were any safer with Karin around. A vampire's bite was lethal and Evan didn't want to have to kill one of Hades's minions because she forgot whose side she was on.

Artemis woke struggling for breath. She gasped, but her lungs wouldn't work, as if a twenty-pound weight lay on her chest. Beside her, Evan jumped into her line of sight. "What is it?"

Grabbing at her chest, she scanned the room, but for what she didn't know. The bedroom door blew open and she met Ash's wide-eyed stare. Her daughter let out a harsh curse and ran to her.

Artemis lifted a hand and started to panic. Her skin appeared paper thin, blue veins clearly visible underneath the surface. Her body shook.

"Apollo, I summon you!" The fear in Ash's voice as she summoned her uncle spiked Artemis's panic and her heartbeat pounded in her ears. Her twin appeared and met her stare. The terror within his blue gaze made her cry. Tears streamed uncontrollably down her face.

Apollo sat on the edge of bed and took her face in

his hands. "Close your eyes and focus on my voice. You must calm down."

She nodded and tried to obey. *What has happened to me, brother?*

"Shh. Don't speak or think." He pressed a hand to her chest bone. "Slowly take a breath in."

When she did, he counted down from five. "Exhale slow."

The panic faded and it became easier to breathe. When Apollo removed his hand, she opened her eyes and focused on his face. He shook his head and pressed a finger to her lips. "You've been poisoned. Do you know who could have done it?"

Artemis shook her head, but Ash answered for her. "No. After arriving by boat, we came straight here."

Apollo pursed his lips and stood. "Why do I smell a vampire?"

Ash folded her arms and glared at her uncle. "Karin is with us."

"That *vamp* is insane. Why is she here?"

The vampire in question entered the room and leaned against the wall next to the bathroom. "I think I may be offended."

Turning toward Artemis, Apollo handed her a vial. "It's ambrosia. You'll need it the longer you're in this realm. I don't trust Karin, so be careful. Also, find out who poisoned you."

He dematerialized and Artemis glanced down at the vial. A sigh slipped from her lips. When she spoke, her voice sounded soft and husky, "It couldn't have been in the food. We all ate the same things."

Evan scooted closer and drew her into his arms. "It would have to be something strong enough to affect you like that. I'd say airborne, but the rest of us should have been affected too."

"*Mana*, get some rest. Ty and I will search the boat and see what we can find." Ash shifted from foot to foot, as if unsure about leaving.

Before Artemis could tell her daughter it was okay, Evan spoke. "She'll be okay. Karin will stay and listen for intruders."

"If anything happens to her, I'm holding both of you accountable." Ash whirled around and left the room.

Artemis settled into Evan's arms and smiled. Ash was her kickass daughter. "I wonder where she gets her attitude?"

A low chuckle rumbled from Evan. "I have no idea, but I think her mother has a temper as well."

"You're not funny."

He kissed her neck. "I'm being serious. Besides, I've always liked your spunk." He fell quiet for a moment. "How are you feeling?"

"Better now." *Thanks to Ash summoning Apollo.* He was the god of disease and prophecy, after all. Somehow, Artemis knew the poison couldn't have killed her. It was meant to slow her down. Only one person would want her out of the way for a few days and be cruel enough to not care if she lived or died. *Hera.*

And Artemis would have been out of commission for days…if Ash hadn't called Apollo.

ASH BOARDED the yacht and searched for anything out of place, anything she might have missed during their trip to the island. Much to her annoyance, everything had been cleaned. All the glasses they'd used were gone, as was the fruit tray.

With a growl, she turned and ran into Ty's hard chest. He gripped her elbows, drawing her attention to his face before he lifted his shades, resting them on top of his head. "Nothing onboard this ship made Artemis ill."

She placed her hands on his chest and tapped on finger against his pecs. "Why didn't you tell me?"

His lips twisted, then one side of his sensual mouth lifted. "Because I needed to talk to Ares."

"You…" She poked him in the chest. "…need to communicate a little more."

Lowering his head, he nipped at her ear and she groaned. "You are too stubborn. Plus you were so pissed because someone poisoned your mother. I let you walk it off."

If it had been anyone else, she'd have kicked his ass. She still might do so later. Jerking out of his hold, she crossed her arms. "Is dear old dad on his way?"

"Dad is here." Ares's deep voice sent a shiver up her spine, but she dismissed it and faced the god of war.

Ty lowered his shades back in place and spoke before she could get a smart ass comment out. "Artemis was poisoned."

"I didn't do it."

Ash took a step forward, but Ty grabbed her by the waist with one arm. "Would your mother do it?"

A dry laugh escaped Ares. "Of course she would, but did she? Not sure."

"Do you know where she is?"

"Yes."

Ash let out a huff and jerked against Ty's tight hold. "Ares! Where the hell is she?"

The god narrowed his gaze at Ash. She straightened her spine, ready for whatever he might dish out. However, he didn't react to her defiance. Instead, he turned his attention back to Ty and answered the question. "Hera has a mountainside home on the north end of the island." Then he dematerialized.

"Damn him." She faced Ty, hands on her hips.

He hooked an arm around her and yanked her against him. "You really need to learn to have a little patience, goddess."

Before she could reply, he crushed his mouth to hers. His tongue pushed through the seam of her lips seeking hers. She hopped up and wrapped her legs around his waist. The next thing she knew, her back touched cool sheets.

Breaking the kiss, she glanced around and smiled as she noticed it was their room back at the hotel. She removed his sunglasses and tossed them on the nightstand, then rose to kiss the scars on the right side of his face. "I love you, my dragon."

"Love you always, my huntress."

She laughed and drew back to stare into his eyes. With his shades gone, it felt like she was talking to both the man and the dragon. It pleased her to see both sides at once. The right eye—the dragon's eye—was a shade darker red than the scales of his beast with gold flecks scattered throughout the irises. The pupil narrowed into a thin elongated slit right before Ty telekinetically removed their clothes and entered her with a quick thrust, stretching her, filling her.

Tingles scattered over her too-sensitive skin. Pleasure built as Ty pulled out and entered her over and over, each thrust harder and faster than the prior one. She dragged her nails against his back and rode the wave of orgasm as it crashed over her. Ty followed her over the edge with a roar.

CHAPTER EIGHT

"Feeling better?"

Artemis glanced up from the tablet she had tried to figure out for the last hour and met Evan's concerned stare. Setting the device down, she held out her hands to him. "Much better."

He took her hands and sat in the chair next to her. Nodding to the tablet, he asked, "What are you doing?"

"Trying to figure out how to bring up a map. Ash said Hera has a house on the north end of the island. She also mentioned something about an earth app that gives you satellite images." She drew her brows together and studied the thing. I didn't make any sense to her.

He bit his lip as if hiding a smile. Turning the device, he began tapping things on the screen. A moment later, an image of the island appeared. A couple more taps and the image zoomed in, showing the northern mountains.

"You will have to teach me to use this device someday."

"Deal." He leaned in and kissed her.

Heat flooded her body, pushing her closer to him. She threaded her fingers into his hair and opened to allow his tongue to dance with hers. A clearing of a throat made her break the kiss and glare at Ty and Ash as they entered the shared sitting area between their rooms.

Ash stopped at the table and noted the tablet. "Oh good, you got the map up."

Ty turned a chair backward and straddled it. "I think the best thing would be for you two to teleport right in front of the house because Hera is expecting you. Ash and I will teleport about fifty feet from the house in case you need us. I don't trust the female."

Ash laughed and ran her fingers through her mate's hair. "There aren't very many you do trust, dear."

Evan closed his hand over Artemis's. "I'm ready to get this over with, but are we sure she's even there?"

"I just got back from there. She's home," Ash said.

Straightening, Artemis pushed away the hint of anxiety threating to rise. "Let's go then."

The others nodded, stood, and together they teleported to about fifty feet from the house. It was a modest home for Hera's standards. Painted white with brown trim, it was three stories high, with two ivory columns on either side of the front porch.

Taking a deep breath, Artemis grabbed Evan's hand

and began walking toward the house. The closer they got, the more she sensed the thick magic in the air. The god queen must've warded the place against intruders. Worry churned in Artemis's, since Hera had never been the most stable goddess. The jealously she held against Leta, Artemis's mother, had passed down to her. Artemis and Apollo were Zeus' children from his first marriage, a marriage Hera ended so she could have the god king for herself.

When they got within a few feet of the porch, the door opened and Hera stepped out, a scowl on her face. "You are not welcome here. I suggest you leave."

Artemis stood her ground. She took the folded envelop from her pants pocket and held it out. "I've found you, and therefore I deliver this message from Zeus. My mission is complete."

The envelope burst into flames, burning Artemis's fingers. She dropped it and the message dissolved into ash before hitting the ground. Her chest tightened and fury mounted inside her. Fisting her hands, she stepped forward only to have Evan grip her arm.

Hera laughed, throwing her head back. "I never received a message." Then the goddess went back inside, slamming the door behind her.

Artemis conjured her bow and arrows. Evan moved to stand in front her and held onto her arms. "Don't. We'll figure out how to make it work. My god status doesn't matter. We already know I can enter Olympus."

She moved her gaze from the house to Evan and back again. "I still want to kill her."

"I know. I'm sure you're not the only one."

Focusing back on him, she relaxed. Her heart broke for him. He'd been through so much, had so much taken from him. It was unfair.

"Hey." He lifted her chin with a finger so she looked into his emerald eyes. "We have each other. That's all I care about."

She hugged him tight. "Guess there's nothing else to do but go home."

"Which home?"

Not having to think about where she wanted to go with him, she said, "Your home. I don't want to be in Olympus right now."

EVAN MATERIALIZED in his living room with Artemis by his side. They'd said their goodbyes to Ash and Ty before leaving Ikaria. The couple understood he and Artemis need some time to sort things out, details like their living arrangements. As a goddess, Artemis could live on earth for a long period of time, however she also needed to be in her temple in order to keep the balance flowing between the worlds.

She turned to face him. Her eyes shone with tears she refused to let fall. "Make love to me. Make me believe we will be together for the rest of our immortal lives."

He cupped her face and closed the small gap between them. "We *will* be together for eternity. I love you more now than I did fifteen hundred years ago. This time, I'm not giving up or allowing anyone to separate us. I promise you that."

Throwing her arms around him, she squeezed. "I love you, too."

His heart swelled at her words even though, deep down, he'd already known how she felt. Over the past few days, the bond they'd once had reconnected. He scooped her up and carried her to the bedroom.

When he stepped inside the room, Artemis squirmed out of his arms and tugged him to the bed. She pushed him to a seated position and dropped to her knees. There was a slight tremble in her hands as she undid his pants and freed his cock.

Not knowing where he found his patience, he watched her slowly take him into her hand and lower her head to lick the tip of erection. *Fuck.* He nearly jumped up, but managed to hold still. Her warm mouth covered him and he groaned.

Raking a hand through her hair, he gathered it up in a ponytail. She glanced up at him, and it was his undoing. Watching her mouth move over the length of him while her tongue slipped out when she reached the head was too much. He jerked back, sliding his cock out of her mouth, then lifted her to her feet where he jerked up her dress and ripped her panties off.

Laughing Artemis straddled him, easing down onto his impossibly hard and aching cock. Her moist pussy milked him as she rotated her hips. He gripped her ass and moved with her until they cried out at the same time. "Love you always."

"Love you more." She wrapped her legs and arms around him, then bit him.

A sharp sting transformed into pleasure as she began to ride him again. Willing his own small fangs, he brushed her hair from her neck and struck. Gods didn't need to form a blood bond to mate like the dragons, they could simply pledge their love and loyalty. However, a blood bond was unbreakable, making the couple unable to live without the other. Evan was more than happy to form such a bond with Artemis. She was his and he never wanted to be without her again.

CHAPTER NINE

Artemis reached over and dropped the pasta into the boiling water. When she released the dried noodles, hot water splashed up and caught her hand before she could jerk it away. "Fuck."

She rushed to the sink, turned the cold water on, and stuck her hand under the flow. Evan came into the kitchen and glanced around. "What are you doing?"

"I'm trying to cook for you."

He bit his lower lip and moved to turn down the temperature on the burner. "You don't need to learn to cook." Coming up behind her, he wrapped his arms around her waist and kissed her temple. "I don't need a wife who cooks. We are gods by birthright, and we can conjure our food. I cook out of habit from living here for so long. We've been over this."

She closed her eyes and leaned into him, soaking up his warmth. "I know."

Placing his hands on her shoulders, he gently turned her to face him and cupped her head in his hands. "I think it's time we go to Olympus to stay for a few days. It's been two weeks since you've been here. You need to rebuild your power."

"I don't want to go back."

His jaw worked as if trying to gather his patience. Before he spoke, the doorbell rang. "Who the hell?"

He stormed into the living room and Artemis followed, curious who paid them a visit. When she reached the door, she knew. By the concerned look Evan gave her, she figured he knew as well.

Why now? After two weeks of not talking to her or answering her summons, Zeus picked then to show up. Furious, she jerked open the door and glared at her father. "It's too late. I don't want to talk to you."

The god king placed his foot inside the doorway to keep her from shutting it in his face. "I came to apologize."

She stilled and studied the god. Never in her life had she heard him utter those particular words. He was king, and he never apologized to anyone. "Go on."

Zeus took a breath and scanned his surroundings. "May I come in?"

She stepped aside to allow him entrance while Evan disappeared into the kitchen. After a long silence, her father spoke loud enough for Evan to hear. "I revoke the curse I placed on Evangelos and reinstate him as god of messengers. I also give my blessings on the union the two of you have created."

Relief and joy filled her. Her vision blurred as Zeus tugged her into a hug and kissed the top of her head. "I wish the both of you would stay in Olympus, but the choice is yours."

Then he dematerialized.

Artemis stared in disbelief. "I don't understand."

"Ashlynn, I summon you."

A moment later Ash appeared and glared at her father in annoyance. "Seriously?"

"Zeus was here. With no explanation, he reinstated my god status and blessed you mother and me on our union."

A smile lit up her face. "That's great."

Artemis studied her daughter. She was hiding something. "What did you do?"

Wide-eye in a false attempt at innocence, Ash blinked. "I don't know what you are referring to."

"Ashlynn," Evan growled.

Dropping her shoulders, Ash confessed. "I might have gone to Zeus and told him about his wife being an evil bitch, that's all."

"And what happened?" Dread churned in Artemis's gut. Zeus could be the most loyal and caring king and father when he wanted, but pissing him off risked feeling his wrath. "Where is Hera?"

Ash waved a hand and sat on the sofa. "She was there, smug as always. You see she promised Zeus to go in on the journey he sent you two on as a test of your strengths and love, but you guessed it already. Hera decided she didn't want you two together, living in Olympus. To her, it was a way to get rid of 'Zeus's daughter.'"

Evan laughed and dropped in the armchair, pulling Artemis into his lap. "By reinstating me and asking us to come home, he is annoying Hera."

"Yep. Oh, and he has forbidden her to go near either of you. No repercussions are to make it back to you." Ash smiled, making Artemis shiver. "Well, congrats to the two of you. My mate is running me a bubble bath. See ya."

She vanished and Artemis began to giggle, then laughter overtook her until tears ran down her face. "I think I'm finally losing my mind."

Evan hugged her. "It's okay. You're mine, crazy or not. Let's open another bottle of wine and celebrate."

Sobering a little, Artemis kissed him. "That sounds wonderful. We'll return home tomorrow, but I want to keep this place, so we have somewhere to escape."

"Anything you wish, my wife." He framed her face and kissed her. Allowing his lips to linger, he added, "I love you."

"I love you, my husband." She stood and gave him a crooked smile. "Go get the wine and meet me in the bath. Do you have bubbles?"

"Under the sink." He rose to his feet and hooked an

arm around her. "I can't wait to spread bubbles over your body."

Her skin heated and pussy ached. "Let's save the wine for after the bath."

"Deal." He scooped her up and carried her down the hall. Artemis's heart swelled with happiness she hadn't felt in a long time. She had her god back and she wasn't ever letting him go. She bit his ear lobe and whispered, "By the way, I'm pregnant."

NEXT IN THE SONS OF WAR SERIES

CHAOTIC WAR

While Zavier Sullivan may be the calm, reserved brother, his dragon is not. Especially since the beautiful, unorganized demi-goddess, Danielle Roberts—a.k.a Elle—moved into the mansion and into his life. She disturbs his OCD and makes him yearn for things he shouldn't, but he can't stay away from her. Nor can he deny her anything. Including his blood.

Ever since arriving at the home of the Sons of War, Elle has been plagued with dreams of the past and future. The visions are taking a toll, causing her debilitating headaches and ruining her sleep, but she doesn't know what it all means. Her mother, Nyx, the Goddess of Night, has never bothered to show up and explain things to her. Until she arrives and unlocks Elle's powers, promptly transforming her into a half-daimon, half-goddess. Now, Zavier may be her only hope of holding onto her humanity, but can she bond with him after everything she's seen? Especially in the midst of everything the Sons and their mates are going through.

FOR READERS

I thought the Dragons of Ares world couldn't be any more enjoyable to write until I started Artemis's story. Writing about the gods is like a world inside a world. Will there be other short stories about the gods? You bet. Although I can't reveal which god is next or when the next novella will be out, I can tell you it'll be an awesome journey.

The next novel in the series is Chaotic War, Zavier and Elle's story. Thank you so much for making the start of the series a success. I'm overjoyed by the emails and comments from my readers saying how much they love the series and ask for more. Love you guys!

ABOUT LIA DAVIS

Lia Davis is the USA Today bestselling author of more than sixty books, including her fan favorite Ashwood Falls Series.

A lifelong fan of magic, mystery, romance and adventure, Lia's novels feature compassionate alpha heroes and strong leading ladies, plenty of heat, and happily-ever-afters.

Lia makes her home in Northeast Florida where she battles hurricanes and humidity like one of her heroines.

When she's not writing, she loves to spend time with her family, travel, read, enjoy nature, and spoil her kitties.

She also loves to hear from her readers. Send her a note at lia@authorliadavis.com!

Follow Lia on Social Media

Website: http://www.authorliadavis.com/
Newsletter: http://www.
subscribepage.com/authorliadavis.newsletter

Facebook author fan page: https://www.facebook.com/novelsbylia/
Facebook Fan Club: https://www.facebook.com/groups/LiaDavisFanClub/
Twitter: https://twitter.com/novelsbylia
Instagram: https://www.instagram.com/authorliadavis/
BookBub: https://www.bookbub.com/authors/lia-davis
Pinterest: http://www.pinterest.com/liadavis35/
Goodreads: http://www.goodreads.com/author/show/5829989.Lia_Davis

ALSO BY LIA DAVIS

Paranormal Series

Shifters of Ashwood Falls

Bears of Blackrock

Dragons of Ares

Gods and Dragons

Dark Scales Division (Co-written with Kerry Adrienne)

Shifting Magick Trilogy

The Divinities

Witches of Rose Lake

Coven's End (Co-written with L.A. Boruff)

Academy's Rise (Co-written with L.A. Boruff)

Lucifer's War (Co-written with L.A. Boruff)

Singles Titles

First Contact (MM co-written with Kerry Adrienne)

Ghost in the Bottle (co-written with Kerry Adrienne)

Dragon's Web

Royal Enchantment

Marked by Darkness

His Big Bad Wolf (MM)

Their Royal Ash

Tempting the Wolf

Hexed with Sass (part of the Milly Taiden Sassy Ever After World)

Claiming Her Dragons (Part of the Milly Taiden Paranormal Dating Agency)

Contemporaries

Pleasures of the Heart Series

Single Titles

His Guarded Heart (MM)